THE
FLOWER
AND THE
FLAME

FATED:
HADES AND
PERSEPHONE

DRAGONFIRE PRESS

OTHER BOOKS

Fated

The Head and the Heart

The Flower and the Flame

The Sorrow and the Sea

Cursed

The Princess and the Prophecy

The Fallow and the Faint

The Weaver and the Web

THE FLOWER AND THE FLAME

FATED: HADES AND PERSEPHONE

KERRI KEBERLY

The Flower and the Flame
Copyright © 2024 by Kerri Keberly

Cover design by Keith Robinson

Dragonfire Press

Print ISBN: 978-1-958354-70-4

CHAPTER 1

HADES HAD GROWN accustomed to living in darkness. In fact, after ruling over it for so long, he preferred it, which was why he found it so curious he would be drawn to such light. That time after time he would venture out of the shadows and into the land of the living just to catch a glimpse of it. So radiant, so warm, so bright.

But here he was, yet again.

He cocked his head, staring at her from the shadows, the girl with the sky in her eyes and the flowers in her hair. To her, he appeared as an enormous black wolf, cautiously watching from a distance. How long had it been since her singing had stopped him in his tracks one early summer morning? At least two full moons now.

Though he never hid, he was careful not to stray too far into the meadow in which she picnicked or gathered flowers. It was true the shadowy tree line concealed his dark fur, but she always knew when he was there.

She would smile when she tried to coax him out, to come closer to her. The other forest animals went to her without much convincing at all, and he longed to be near her just as they did, but that would not end well. She might see his eyes, and how they held the same piercing intensity whether he took the shape of a wolf or a man.

A god.

He also might be tempted to speak. Though shrouded in a cloak of fur and claw, a wolf capable of speech would surely give away his immortal identity. He could not have that. The King of the Underworld was not favored among the goddesses of Olympus. As maddening as it was how they made their assumptions about him, there was nothing to be done. If they chose to see fire and flames in his eyes, fury in his heart instead of loneliness, then what could he do?

So, he relied upon the dark gazing pool in his realm, waiting for its magical reflection to show him when the goddess with hair the color of sunlight had entered the meadow once again. On those days he would shift into a wolf, coming up from below to sit and watch as she laughed and sang with the nymph companions her mother, Demeter, goddess of the harvest, had commanded to keep watch over her.

Hades doubted the task was a difficult one. He found Persephone to be an utter delight, not only to gaze upon, but to listen to. She sang often, and it had been her voice that had first caught his attention, while on one of his rare trips above ground. He could not remember the reason for his sojourn. Most likely some matter on Olympus, or perhaps it had simply been a whim for cooler air, but he'd heard Persephone before he saw her, voice like the freshest of breezes. When he did see her, that smile, oh how it shined brighter than Helios.

He whined, low and pitiful, the urge to go to her growing unbearable. He wondered how long he would be able to keep up this charade when a thought came to mind. Perhaps he should try disguising himself as an ordinary man. A passerby on his way to some temple. At least that way he could get closer to her. He could speak to her, if only to ask for directions to the nearest *polis*, or some other menial thing. A whimper caught in his throat, his contemplation overwhelming him. Having had enough torture for the day, he rose quietly, turning so he could head back to his domain undetected.

Persephone stopped singing, and then, quite unexpectedly, he heard her say, "Oh, do not go yet, my friend."

Hades froze, torn between darting away and bolting towards her. Ever so slowly, he turned his massive head in her direction. She took a step forward, hands clasped together just below her throat, no doubt hoping this would be the day that she would finally convince the black wolf to come to her.

The nymphs looked on for a moment—some in horror, some in dismay—before managing to shake themselves out of their stupor. When she leaned forward, as though to take a step, they grasped and pulled on her arms, desperate to stop her from advancing any further.

Hades knew the fear squeezing the air from the lungs in their chests was from the hope that today would *not* be the day their mistress made friends with a giant beast. Demeter was fiercely protective of her daughter, and if Persephone were to be torn apart by an unnaturally large black wolf under their care, they would surely suffer a most terrible consequence. He must go, lest Persephone break free from their clutching hands and come to him.

Before he turned to leave, Hades raised his muzzle into the air and let out a long and suffering howl, even though there was no moon or a single star in sight.

Hades sat upon his throne, restless and possessing no knowledge of anything he could do to ease his torment. His seat of power was grand, carved of obsidian veined with pure gold. The room itself was large enough to accommodate a company of soldiers, yet its dark stone walls somehow seemed to be closing in on him.

Several days had passed, and he had tried to leave Persephone to her dancing and singing, to life as she knew it. Pure and peaceful. But knowing she was there, gracing the world above with her beauty and light, drove him to madness. It seemed he was doomed to dwell in the darkness; in a world where light did not exist. This did more than drive him mad, it haunted him.

He shifted when a swirling black mist rose from the tiled floor, blending into the surrounding darkness. Had it not been for the hammered copper braziers and elaborate chandelier to illuminate his surroundings, Hades wouldn't have noticed it at all.

There was a grand stone arch through which all visitors entered, yet Hecate, goddess of magic, the night, and the moon, chose to appear directly before him.

Like Hades, Hecate was neither benevolent or malevolent, yet carried with her a reputation that made gods and man alike quake at the mere thought of her. All except Hades, for Hecate and he were kindred spirits, and she often visited him in the Underworld to give him counsel.

"Receiver of Many," she greeted, floating closer. Her raven hair rippled in an unseen wind, the pointed ends of her black gown twisting and reaching like tentacles. "I do not think I have ever seen you so distressed. What vexes you?"

"Unrequited love, Hecate," replied Hades, not bothering to hide the truth from the witch. "Is there anything in existence more torturous?"

"Love? For whom?" asked Hecate.

"Persephone, daughter of Zeus and Demeter."

"I see," said Hecate. "A most difficult situation, then, for the ruler of death and darkness to long for one who brings such life and light."

Another confession poured out of him, unbidden. "I appear to her as a wolf when she is with her nymphs in the meadow, just to be near her. I can think of nothing else."

"Ah! Then she does not know of your love."

6

Hades slumped further down into the plush cushion of his throne. "I have not had the courage to tell her my darkness pines after her light, so she does not. And what would she do if she did? Is there any above or below who have not heard of the terrible god Hades? The sinister purveyor of death. Tell me, who does not cower in fear at even the thought of my name?"

Hades pushed himself up and stalked over to an ornate granite fountain holding a pool of still, dark water.

"I see." Hecate glided to where he stood, the rolling fog that forever accompanied her moving with her. "The judgement that you should preside over the souls of the dead has caused you to lose as much as you've gained. But, after all that has been said and done, you are still a king. You can simply take the girl for your own."

"There would be no honor in that," replied Hades, not giving the witch any more leave to fill his head with terrible ideas. Ones that would not bode well for his already infamous reputation, which existed thanks to the unfounded presumption that he was the perpetrator of many diabolical offenses.

"Always one so willing to suffer in the name of honor, Hades. I fear following rules, giving respect where it is oftentimes undue, is the sole source of your misery."

Had she not heard the words that had come out of his mouth?

"I do not wish to frighten her, or force upon her a life she does not want."

"I have looked where no one else has dared," Hecate continued, "into that black depth, and I have found a warm and caring soul in you, Receiver, though your mind broods over the careless misdeeds of gods and man. So misunderstood are you."

She grew larger in size, cresting like a dark wave before breaking into a cascade of smoke, and the whisper of *I know the feeling* echoed in Hades' ears as her ghostly figure reassembled to hover beside him.

Hecate looked down into the same dark pool, at the same image of Persephone as he did now, and said, "It is wise to let her choose. But first she must have something from which to make her choice. Love cannot grow from nothing. There must be soil in which to plant the seed. Go to her, offer her your heart, black as it may be, for the most fertile ground is always the darkest."

Hades contemplated this as he watched Persephone's reflection splash in a stream, laughing and giggling with sheer delight. Would he steal her happiness just so that he may find his?

"Speaking of honor," murmured Hecate, interrupting his thoughts, yet again. Clearly, the witch was not done with the conversation. "Has the great and powerful Zeus given you what you are owed for so steadfastly governing those who no longer walk the Earth?"

Hades shook his head. "I have not yet asked for his word to be honored."

Zeus had promised him a bride long ago, when Hades had agreed to rule over the dead. He hadn't wanted such a realm, one of darkness and despair, but he hadn't had a choice. Poseidon had already been granted the seas, and Zeus, of course, had claimed the heavens and Earth for his own. What was left for the third brother but to rule over imprisoned Titans and the souls of the dead?

"You have a good heart, Hades. You deserve a queen who lights it afire. Perhaps it is time for that brother of yours to make good on his debt," said Hecate before vanishing, leaving no trace she had ever been there except for a curling wisp of smoke.

CHAPTER 2

THE SUN WARMED Persephone's pale skin, and she inhaled the scent of wildflowers—green and tender and fresh—she held in her hand as she stared into the forest.

Day after day, she had gone to the meadow hoping to catch a glimpse of the black wolf. All she saw now were the vibrant hues of spring. Long green grass moved in the breeze, the dots of delicate blues and bursts of white and yellow swaying with it. As always, songbirds chirped their cheerful tune, and the buzz of a nearby hive, from which they would sometimes collect honey, filled the air.

But the wolf was not there.

In fact, she hadn't seen the wolf sitting in its usual spot for nearly a fortnight. Had the mournful howl when she'd seen it last been its final farewell? It saddened her to think so, but she could not dwell in sadness for long, for the most cherished of all her nymph companions, Kyane, approached.

"The beast has not come today." She tugged on Persephone's elbow. "Let us go back to the others. They wish to go downstream and frolic."

Persephone's gaze dropped, her shoulders sinking with it. A moment later, she lifted her head and handed Kyane the flowers. "It is my friend, as all flora and fauna, and it will come again. I know it will, and I will rejoice in the moment it allows me to scratch behind its wild ears."

Kyane nodded at the reproach before linking an arm with Persephone and leading her back toward the others. It was a patronizing gesture, Kyane's nod, but it did not irritate Persephone for long. She found letting go of anger was the wiser choice. The happiness of living in the moment was all that truly mattered.

She wished her mother could do the same. How different they were. Where Demeter was reluctant to change, Persephone welcomed it. She supposed that was why she was the goddess of rebirth.

She inhaled cheerfully, turning her face up to the cloudless sky and reveling in the warmth of the sun shining down on her. Tomorrow was a new day. The wolf would visit again, she was sure of it. In all the days it had come, it had never prowled or hunted any of them like prey, only sat quietly and watched over them like a protector.

Comforted by this, Persephone reached her free hand down as she walked, brushing her fingertips over the tall grass and making wildflowers bloom in her wake.

The rays of Helios were bright this day, and Persephone sang happily as she tucked daisies into Kyane's curls. The song caught in her throat when a rustling came from the woods on the other side of the stream.

Both Persephone and Kyane stilled, their heads turning toward the sound at the same time. It was not the wolf as she had hoped, but a hooded figure sitting atop an enormous black horse. The nymphs splashing in the water farther down the stream froze, and when the stranger and his steed stepped out of the shadows and into the dappled sunlight, they scattered, shrieking as they ran.

"I mean no harm," the man called out, putting a hand up as a show of goodwill.

Persephone remained silent, and after a moment or two, the man dismounted. He swung down with graceful ease before pulling back his hood, revealing dark curling hair that brushed the line of his bearded jaw.

Tall and in prime fighting trim, he was dressed in a dark tunic with golden clasps, and the girdle around his waist was made of finely embossed leather. It was plain to see the man was wealthy. But where was his sword? It was unusual for a man of such means to travel without one. Unless, of course, he preferred a hidden dagger to protect him.

"Who are you?" snapped Kyane, standing abruptly. A shower of daisies fell from her hair as she turned to wrap Persephone in a protective embrace. "And what do you want?"

Heat flushed Persephone's face at Kyane's rudeness. She didn't condone it, but she did understand. Such questions should be asked, for if he was in no need to fill his coin purse by theft, then what else was he looking to take by force?

Persephone bit the inside of her lip, hoping the sting of it would convince her heart to stop beating so wildly. Her mother had plenty to say about men. They were boastful, selfish, and brazen enough to ravish nymphs. If this were true, what would stop them from aiming their lustful arrows at a goddess?

"I am Eubulus," said the man. "I say again, I mean you no harm. I am on a search for Demeter's temple." His voice was deep and smooth, and Persephone's heart gathered speed as he walked over to the edge of the stream. "I stopped to fill this..." He held up a water skin. "When I happened upon you. Your voice is beautiful."

Persephone's belly dipped as her mind stretched to the outer reaches of her memory. Not only at the compliment, but because she had heard that name before. It meant *giver of good counsel*. Had she heard it discussed among the gods? Had this man's great wealth attracted their attention somehow? Had they bestowed upon him the ability to walk and talk among them in return for some great or pious deed he had done?

Could he be a hero?

He wasn't forceful in any way, and she did not detect ill intent. Moreover, there was something familiar about the way this man carried himself. It was almost regal. Almost as if he were a prince or a king or... a god.

But Persephone knew every god. She had spoken to, or at least seen, all of them, even the lesser gods like Pan and Zephyrus. All except one... Could it be?

Kyane spoke up once again, scattering Persephone's thoughts.

"Demeter does not have a temple," said Kyane, impatience sharpening her tone. "She receives her sacrifice in the fields, after harvest. Everyone knows that."

"You are right, my lady. I misspoke. Forgive me."

The man struggled with his thoughts for a moment, opening and closing his mouth as though he were about to say something. As though thinking better of the whole conversation, the man turned on his heel to leave.

Persephone's heart raced again, though she was not entirely sure it was out of fear. The way he moved had a familiarity to it. So much so that it made her want to know more about him.

"Where are you from, kind sir?"

Kyane dug her fingers into the soft flesh of Persephone's arms. "Hush! How do you know he is kind? It's best to let him go."

"Honestly, Kyane," whispered Persephone, trying not to be too harsh but failing. "Do you take my mother's word that all men are evil so seriously?" She shrugged out of Kyane's painful grip and took a step toward the man standing on the other side of the stream.

He turned his head toward her slowly, his gaze so intense it rose the fine hairs on her arms. There was something about his eyes that hypnotized her.

"South of here," he replied, facing her once again. "My kingdom has seen great bounty in years past. I only wish to pay homage to the goddess who has blessed me, so that I may have another successful harvest."

Persephone grinned as she drew closer to the edge of the stream, until only the gurgling water separated them. His kingdom? *South* of here? Was she reading too much into his words? Or were they clues to his identity?

The playful arch of his brow certainly made it seem as though either one could be true.

"Yes, then you do look for my mother, Demeter. However, she cannot be found in the spring meadow, but in the field at harvest, and it is much too early for a sacrifice. Only I, her daughter, Persephone, can be found this time of year. Are you sure it was Demeter you were in search of?"

"Ah! The fair Persephone, goddess of spring." The man bowed low. "I am honored."

He had danced around her question, but Persephone didn't press him to answer it. In fact, the brilliance of his smile before he bowed his head succeeded in stealing her breath, making it difficult to form words, much less conduct an interrogation.

She wanted to talk with him more, but not with Kyane or the other nymphs there. For the first time ever, she wished she was alone. "I will tell her of your quest to find her temple, so that you may offer your thanks. I am sorry you traveled all this way for nothing. Will you come back to make a sacrifice?"

Kyane came up behind her suddenly, and Persephone flinched when the nymph said, "You look wealthy enough. Perhaps you should build a temple to Demeter in addition to your sacrifice."

The man continued to look at Persephone with his enchanting dark gaze, piercing through her calm demeanor with astonishing speed. "Perhaps I should also build a temple in homage to you, fair Persephone, and offer my kingdom as a sacrifice," he said, a knowing smile on his lips.

Persephone's cheeks warmed. Of all the days she'd spent enjoying the natural beauty that Gaia had to offer, all the joyous splendor, all the wondrous flora and fauna, she had never experienced anything quite like what she felt now.

Kyane rolled her eyes before scoffing loudly. "Go away, *kind sir*. You are not wanted here," she said, turning away in disgust. "Come,

Persephone. We have better things to do than waste our time on flattery."

Persephone pressed her lips together, torn between obeying Kyane, who she knew was only being gruff to protect her honor, and listening to her heart.

Her heart won.

This was no ordinary man. He was a god, and if Persephone's hunch was right, one of three powerful brothers.

"Go Kyane. I will be there in a moment."

Kyane eyed her suspiciously, her gaze cutting between Persephone and the man before she finally headed toward the others.

Persephone spoke fast and low, so that Kyane and the other nymphs huddling together nearby did not hear her words. "I believe you are a king, though not a mortal one traveling unarmed and alone. You are a god, for only gods would be so brazen to approach a goddess, let alone speak to one." Her pulse jumped in her throat. Reckless, she was being reckless, throwing caution to the wind and hoping she would not be sorry. "Meet me here under the cover of darkness, so that we may discuss the details of why you have traveled *north* of your kingdom."

The man smiled again, with such brightness that Persephone thought she might faint. "You are as perceptive as you are beautiful, goddess. I will come."

Persephone turned away quickly, darting with light feet over to the waiting nymphs before her legs could give out. And before she thought better of what she'd done and changed her mind.

CHAPTER 3

EVEN WITH THE moonlight glinting off the water, the stream looked as though it were the darkest of ink running over the rocks. Persephone had never seen the world in this light; the absence of it, to be more accurate. She simply hadn't given it a thought to look upon the forest through the eyes of the moon after the sun had gone down, and she regretted it, for the darkness painted as beautiful a picture as the light did.

She gazed at the full moon, its silvery light as capable of creating shadows as the sun, and then turned her head to spy an owl nestled in a nearby tree, watching her discoveries with wide and knowing eyes.

Persephone pulled her cloak tighter around her shoulders, supposing the bird had a right to its gloating stare. Only a fool would think such a difference of perspective did not exist. She was a little embarrassed it had taken her this long to see it.

A faint rustling set her on edge, and she stood straighter, assuming a more commanding position, as a goddess without the safety net of her nymph companions must do. When a fox stepped out of the darkness, head bent low and wary, she relaxed. It sniffed the ground as it walked, cautious and ready to run should she make any sudden movement.

Persephone knelt slowly, beckoning the animal to her with an outstretched arm, an open hand offering the promise of a gentle touch. The fox crept closer, and with every soothing sound she made, its ears pricked forward with curiosity instead of lying flat with fear. When it was finally close enough, the fox not only allowed her to pet its head, but also smooth down the hackles standing along its back.

"He likes you."

Persephone gasped, standing so quickly the fox darted into the shadows, yelping as it fled. She did the best she could to calm her breathing, for she did not want to admit she had been just as startled as the animal. But the man had approached so silently—so suddenly—it had unnerved her.

It shouldn't have, for this was the way of gods.

"And I him," she replied, trying to keep a satisfied smirk from overtaking her face. He

21

was a god, not a man, and she was sure of it now that he had given himself away.

He kept his distance, nodding his head and paying respect to her before speaking. "I am happy to see you again, goddess."

"And I you," Persephone replied, offering him a slight dip of her head. In truth, she did not know if it was a good or bad idea to meet an unknown god like this, alone in the dark. Yet, she could not deny the thrill it gave her to see him again, even if it was only to confirm her suspicion.

To carry on with the coy game they were playing.

But she had started it, hadn't she? Asking him to meet her alone like this for a thrill. In her defense, her mother had kept so much from her, was it any wonder she found the company of strangers new and exciting?

She demurely cleared her throat. "Let us sit by the water's edge, shall we?"

"Of course, my goddess," he replied. "Lead the way and I shall follow."

Less complicated than her reasons for meeting him under the cover of night, she found she was simply enthralled with the sound of his voice. He could babble like an infant, she supposed, and she would listen for hours, perhaps even days. So, Persephone found a comfortable spot near the stream and sat, close enough so that she could dip her fingers into the water. He sat beside her, resting his arms on his knees. Their presence stirred the forest inhabitants, and no sooner had they sat, a round of soft chirping and chatty clicking began.

"Shall we start with your true name?" asked Persephone.

He laid a hand on the ground. A snake slithered from the grass and into his palm. "Eubulus, giver of..."

Persephone stopped swirling her fingers in the water. His trust was proving just as difficult to coax out of him as it had been the wolf. She straightened at this thought, looking the man in his moon-lit eyes.

"Good counsel, I know," replied Persephone. "Although I enjoy our game, it is time to tell me the truth of who you are. You are no mortal."

He remained silent, letting the snake uncoil itself from his arm and be on its way. After a moment longer, he inhaled deeply, blowing out a long breath before answering.

"You are right, Persephone, I am no mortal." He hesitated, as if his next words caused him pain. "I am Hades." He averted his gaze by lifting his head toward the moon. "King of the Underworld, Receiver of Many, Guardian of the Dead."

She remained silent as she studied his features. He was more handsome than she imagined he would be. The way the others spoke of him, she would have thought he would be hideous, with protruding cheekbones and a sharply hooked nose. It was quite the opposite. In fact, he was so pleasing to her that she found she could not look away.

"Am I not the daemon you expected, goddess?" he said with a laugh.

"I'm sorry. It's rude to stare. I just..."

"No, no. I'm flattered. And I must say, you are a vision of loveliness yourself, especially under the moon like this. Believe me when I say I have half a mind to build a temple made of the finest marble in your honor."

Her heart raced again. "I require no temple, only enlightenment. I fear my mother has kept me sheltered for far too long. I am quite embarrassed to have thought you a beast."

"Oh, I can be, there is no doubt about that," he replied, the barest hint of a smile curling his lips.

She knew he still toyed with her. He had admitted who he was, but now there was something else he was hiding.

"A beast you say?" she continued, feeling more at ease with each moment that passed. "A fearsome thing with claws and fangs..."

"I would not say fearsome," he said, shaking his head.

"What would you say then?"

"Protective."

Persephone gasped, though not out of fear. She was the furthest thing from afraid. She was amazed. Astounded that he had divulged so easily.

"The wolf. It was you?"

He nodded, dropping all pretense. "I heard you singing one day while I was on my way back to the Underworld. I stopped my chariot, so that I could find the source of such divine sound. When I saw you, I was instantly captivated."

She tilted her head at him, taking stock of his words. Turning them over in her mind, she weighed them against the trust that had already grown within her.

"Then why would you not come to me?"

"And scare your nymphs?" he replied. "I am many things, but I am no fool. You saw how they reacted when I approached you as a man."

"They are skittish, yes, but surely you have heard of the savage acts committed against women, especially women as beautiful as nymphs?"

"I have, which is why I chose to keep my distance. I could not keep it for long, however. Believe me when I say that I have never laid eyes on such beauty before. As I've said, I am enthralled with you. But how can the king of darkness approach such a light when his reputation as one who would snatch life away without just cause precedes him?"

"He cannot," whispered Persephone, her heart bursting open, flooding her with sadness and joy at the same time. "He must watch from the shadows as a great black wolf."

Hades said nothing, only looked into her eyes with an earnestness that only the purest of heart could possess. Could it be true Hades was not the monster the gossiping goddesses on Olympus made him out to be?

From what she had experienced of him so far, he was nothing of the sort. Besides being pleasant to look at, he was courteous and kind, understanding and patient, even a bit playful. When he smiled, so did she, for his high spirit was contagious.

No, Hades was nothing like his tempestuous brothers. They were careless with their power, philandering, and worst of all, needlessly cruel sometimes simply because they could be.

Like the fireflies dotting the night around them, their soft glows pulsing like heartbeats, the truth made Persephone's own heart alight with something more than physical attraction. She had grown fonder and fonder of Hades since the first moment she'd laid eyes on him, more than she had expected she would.

"What is it?" asked Hades.

She smiled, adding perceptive to the list of reasons she could not deny she wanted to see him again even if she tried.

"I rather like getting to know who you are, Hades," she replied. "Shall we meet here the same time tomorrow?"

The grin that took over his face told her everything she needed to know.

She made to stand up, for the time to go had come. Hades was quick to help her to her feet.

"Perhaps I might even see you before then, in the light of day." His hands were warm, his nearness intoxicating. It made her heart quicken, and the realization suddenly hit her that she didn't think she could wait even that long. "I promise to leave you to your altruism."

Hades lifted one of her hands to his lips and gently kissed the back of it, causing the butterflies in her stomach to flutter. "Anything for you, goddess."

CHAPTER 4

PERSEPHONE WALKED BESIDE her mother through a field of golden wheat. Harvest season was almost upon them, which meant sacrifices would soon take place. Demeter could often be found in the fields during this time, inspecting each stalk and blessing each kernel. The finest, most abundant crops yielded the best sacrifices.

"Mother?" A gentle breeze lifted Persephone's hair, which was a shade lighter than her mother's burnished tresses but no less sun-kissed.

"Yes, Kore?"

Persephone's smile at the term of endearment was tight. Her mother often called her "the maiden," and it had been fine when she was younger. Now that she was older, it didn't quite fit. As a youth, she had been taught how to use her power to awaken a blade of grass or coax a reluctant bud to bloom, but not much of the world beyond that.

She would have been content to only know that had she not seen how Ares was drawn to Aphrodite, like the honeybee is to a flower's sweet nectar.

If she had never set eyes on Hades.

A maiden. Persephone supposed it was what her mother intended to keep her, but it wasn't what she wished to remain. Her many clandestine meetings with Hades since that very first night had awoken something in her, and she wished to understand it, to know the name for what she felt.

"What does it mean when you miss someone when they are away? When you wish to be near them always?"

Demeter let go of a handful of wheat to look at her. "Fear not, daughter, Kyane and the nymphs will always be near. You shall have no reason to miss them." After a moment, she narrowed her amber eyes the slightest bit, another possibility for Persephone's questions dawning in them.

"Why do you ask me this?"

Persephone reached for a clump of wilted stalks, damaged from a pelting rain or the trampling hooves of an animal. Her fingertips tingled as her magic turned time back on itself and the broken wheat mended, leaving tender green shoots in her grasp.

"Because I wish to know."

Her mother blew a short breath from her nose as she took the repaired stalks into her own hand. Persephone watched as her mother's magic turned them golden brown and nearly ready for harvest.

"Does this have to do with the stranger who Kyane told me caught you most unaware during a frolic in the meadow some months ago?"

How to answer? Persephone could not find it in her heart to lie, especially to her mother, a most stern goddess when angered. She had never been the source of her mother's wrath, but she had seen the consequence of it when Demeter's fellow Olympians had stirred her. It was a most terrible and dreadful time, and Persephone did not like to see her mother in such a state. To calm her on the days she returned from Zeus's council room angered, Persephone would delight her mother with blooms, soothing her with the best, most breathtaking displays.

"Do not worry yourself over that, Mother," replied Persephone, trying her best to sound nonchalant. "He was only passing through."

Despite Persephone's careful words, her mother's temper had been sparked.

"Kyane said you spoke with him privately. What could a goddess possibly have to say to a mortal?" she said sternly, giving Persephone a sideways glance as they continued walking.

Persephone steeled herself, so that the first lie she'd ever told her mother sounded believable. "I reminded him to whom he owes a sacrifice. Without the grain to sustain his people and his livestock, he would not be so wealthy. I told him it was gracious Demeter to whom he must give thanks."

Her flattery worked, and Demeter softened. "Oh, Persephone. What a loyal daughter are you. So pure-hearted and kind, my child."

This version of her mother did not last long.

"But make no mistake, whomever he was, he came under false pretenses," continued Demeter. "To catch a glimpse of a divine breast, or perhaps abduct a nymph for his own selfish pleasure. Lustful, depraved, and deceitful, whether they be god or mortal, all men are the same and I bid you to stay well away from them. Kyane was right to send him away."

Persephone did not speak, for she knew there was nothing she could do or say to change her mother's mind once it was set.

The truth of the matter was that Hades, feared lord of the dark by all, *had* been deceitful. Even if his heart had been in the right place, even if Persephone could explain, her mother would never listen, and would most surely use his actions as evidence to bolster her claim that all men were not to be trusted.

No, Persephone would not find the answers she sought about love and longing from her mother. And she could understand, for her mother's heart had been broken, her honor carelessly stolen, and her maidenhood selfishly taken by Persephone's father, Zeus.

"I do not wish to be harsh, Kore," her mother continued in a gentler tone. "But I know of no other way to make you understand. If anything were to happen to you, should harm befall you in any way, should sorrow consume you and blacken your dear and precious heart, I could not live with myself. You are the one thing in this world that brings me joy, my beloved daughter. I do all things to protect you."

CHAPTER 5

HADES' GAZE DROPPED from the crescent moon hanging in the night sky to the goddess sitting beside him. His heart raced in his chest as he surveyed the soft curves of her face, the graceful arch of her throat.

He took her hand in his, and she abandoned her quiet stargazing to look at him. When her eyes found his, his lungs seized, and he found himself holding his breath as he so often did around her.

He exhaled, then lifted her hand to his lips, pressing a kiss to the back of it. "Tell me what you are thinking. I wish for there to be no secrets between us."

"Is it a secret that Eros possesses one less golden arrow?" She squeezed his hand once before lifting it to her chest and placing it over her heart.

A smile curled the corners of his mouth. No, it was no secret. "Two less golden arrows."

The beating he felt beneath his palm began to quicken, and his own heart responded in kind, matching its mate in intensity. He moved to caress her cheek, and when she did not shy

34

away, he cupped her face in his hands and drew her closer to him.

A brilliance flashed behind his eyes when their lips met, and in that moment, so sweet and chaste and pure, he saw an image of them running together through a meadow dotted with flowers. When she threaded her fingers into his hair, pulling him closer and opening her mouth to him, the image in his mind changed.

They lay entwined in the dark.

He may not know much, but there was one thing that was clear. It was impossible for him to continue dwelling alone in darkness without her. The time had come. He could wait no longer to know if she felt the same.

He broke the kiss, laying his forehead on hers and asking breathlessly, "Would you be my queen if I asked?"

She closed her eyes, inhaling a shaking breath before opening them again to look at him through a watery gaze. He thought she might be surprised at the question, but he hadn't expected a reaction like this.

"What is it?" asked Hades. "Have I spoken the desire of my heart too soon?"

"My dark king," she began, "you must know that I would be your queen, without hesitation, if I were not torn between following my heart and abandoning my duty."

Hades leaned back, panic squeezing his chest. "What duty is it that holds you in place?"

She shook her head, her face still so exquisite even in the faintest light. "Perhaps duty is not the right word. But what else can I call it?" She looked away, out over the stream and into the dark woods where the crickets sang their song. "It is I, her daughter, that Demeter cherishes above all else. I am a bird who has just discovered she has wings, yet I do not know if I can bear the guilt of leaving that nest which my mother has built around me. I am called by nature to fly but remain flightless out of fear that I may lose sight of the one who made me."

He could find no words to express the depth of his alarm, the breadth of his panic that she might not accept his proposal. Anger began to rise, blowing on the embers of his fear and turning it into a raging inferno. He knew she must have witnessed the change in his eyes, the stiffening of his limbs, and it took every ounce of self-control he had not to cry out in frustration.

"Oh, Hades," she wailed, clutching his arms and holding onto him as if she thought he would get up and walk away before hearing the last of her lament. As if any of it was her fault. "I am weak, caught between preserving her happiness and finding my own, and it feels as though it may tear me apart."

How dare Demeter keep his sweet Persephone bound so tightly to her, selfishly denying her daughter the happiness she herself had never found?

He folded her into his arms, kissing her head and stroking her hair until both her sobbing and his anger subsided. What else could he do? The hatred in his eyes had already scared her enough. He would never forgive himself if he lost control and allowed his anger to take over.

"You think your mother would not want you to be happy?" he asked, softly so she would not detect the resentment for Demeter growing within him.

Persephone straightened, and he wiped away her tears as she answered his question. "I think she would... but I fear her idea of happiness is not the same as mine. She has forbidden me to keep the company of men, and here I am in the arms of one so notorious."

Hades had never regretted ruling the Underworld so much as he did at that moment. Neither could he be more determined to keep Persephone by his side than now. "I will go to

Olympus and profess my love, to both Zeus and Demeter. I will promise to cherish you always, as much and more as the goddess of the harvest herself."

"And if they refuse? If my mother's temper flares and leaves me no choice but to..."

"Shhhh, my sweet and fair Persephone. Zeus cannot deny me, and I will prove to Demeter I am worthy of her daughter's heart. I will go on the morrow, and after I have professed my love, they will see that Fate has already woven our threads together, and the all-knowing sisters' work must not be undone. Wait for me here on the evening of the day after next, and I will come for you."

Persephone smiled, her tears already drying, and kissed him with soft lips before whispering, "Then my answer is yes. I will be your queen."

CHAPTER 6

HADES HAD NOT seen his brother in some time, but within moments of setting eyes upon the ruler of the gods, and hearing the crackling of electricity in the air, he was reminded of the raw power that was Zeus. He was the epitome of strength.

Although Hades did not present as weak in appearance, he knew Zeus, in all his towering glory, thought Hades unequal in that regard. Even so, Hades did not begrudge Zeus his massive stature and bulging muscles. Nor did he regret his brother's resolute sense of self or brash character. If not for those qualities, Hades and the rest of his siblings would be forever trapped inside the dark pit of their treacherous father's belly. It had been the power of Zeus—his unshakeable will, undeniable cunning, and sheer brute force—that had saved them all.

Saved *Hades*.

Yes, his younger brother had come to his rescue, and perhaps that was the real tension that ran between them, a tenuous thread always threatening to snap when tugged too tightly.

What had Hades done except sit silently in the rumbling and gurgling dark? Poseidon had at least caused terrible upset, bellowing while thrashing and pounding at the walls of their prison. Hades had gotten lost in his head, wrapped up in trying to understand the fear that drove their father to consume his children.

Try as he might, Hades could not find an answer, and so resentment had begun to well within him. It had turned to anger, seething and simmering instead of rising and boiling over. He knew full well how impotent he had seemed as he had sat plotting and planning his revenge, quietly rather than through endless but useless wailing and screaming.

After Zeus had liberated the sons and daughters of Cronus, and the titans had been vanquished, he had shown his appreciation by offering his brothers their own kingdoms to rule. When the bowels of the Earth had been given to Hades, he had not fought against it. Cowardice deserved such punishment, for that is how Zeus saw it, and there was no use arguing, for Hades had seen what had become of those who had gone against mighty Zeus.

No, Hades' outrage had not manifested outwardly, and he had forever been marked as less powerful because of it, even though he would argue his nature, his way of handling injustice, was a display of something equally as important: Cunning.

He had hoped that with his strategic contributions during the ten years of battle with the Titans that perception would have been changed. It had not, and it angered him still to this day. But what kind of madman would go against his savior?

There was no shortage of pride among Rhea and Cronus's sons, that was not the issue. In fact, ego had Hades on the verge of constantly trying to explain his ever-present brooding. But he had inherited his mother's gentle nature, and it was gratitude for being saved that kept Hades from trying to make his brother understand his dark and contemplative moods.

Hades knew it would have been a waste of breath if he tried explaining why he was caught in his head so much, for he doubted Zeus could comprehend. He rarely contemplated anything, that was evident in the many adulterous affairs in which he engaged, because he was a god of action, with little to no patience for rumination.

Hecate's words came back to him. *So misunderstood are you.* She knew the way of it, and how difficult it was smoothing a dent after the metal had been struck.

None of that mattered this day. This day, all would be forgiven. He would ride down the mountain with the blessing to marry the goddess who loved him as he was, his sweet Persephone, and all would be forgotten.

Hades' footsteps echoed as he passed through the enormous throne room. The space was much lighter than his darkened hall, with polished white marble and sparkling granite from top to bottom. He arched an eye at Zeus's and Hera's thrones, which were both empty, and continued through a backdrop of billowing curtains out onto a veranda.

"Brother!" Zeus raised a hand in greeting. "What brings you to Olympus? What complaint have you to lodge now?" His raucous laughter resounded, even in the large open-aired space.

"No complaints, brother, only a question," replied Hades evenly as he approached Zeus, who was sprawled across a couch, a bevy of beautiful nymphs lounging on pillows at his feet.

Hades did not begrudge Hera her jealousy and anger when it came to Zeus. It seemed he was incapable of fidelity. He was, however, steadfast and loyal.

And king of them all.

Perhaps it is time for that brother of yours to make good on his debt.

It was not so much of a debt as it was a promise. Still, Hades supposed he should not tread already thin ice cloaked in such a heavy and brooding mood.

Yet, he could not help himself from taking his time walking over to a freestanding table that held platters of fruit, bread, and an assortment of olives and soft cheeses. The food was unnecessary, more for aesthetics and pleasure than anything. Zeus never could govern his love of frivolity and excess.

Hades plucked a date from one of the gleaming platters and inspected it, waiting for the right words to fill his head so that they might roll off the tongue easily.

"I see you have not lost your penchant for sulking, Hades. Do not keep me in suspense. What is your question?"

Hades set the date back down onto the plate. The irritation in Zeus's voice was plain. Hades must rein in his petulance if his marriage to Persephone was to be a successful endeavor. "I am only thinking of how to frame the delicate matter of which I wish to speak to you about."

Zeus raised an eyebrow. "And what matter is that?"

"The promise you made when I accepted my fate as ruler of everything below without protest," said Hades, pausing a moment before continuing, "I have come to—"

"Finally! I was beginning to worry about you, Hades. I find it most curious your genitals have not yet exploded from disuse. Which of the goddesses have caught your eye? If it is Artemis, I say now you may want to choose another, she has vowed to forever remain a maiden. Athena is likewise."

"Persephone."

Zeus sat silent and unblinking. The seconds passed, and when he shifted in his chair to stroke his beard, Hades knew the meaning for the contemplation. His brother was deciding whether to call Demeter into the throne room, so that she had a chance to bless or reject the marriage.

The goddess of the harvest looked mild mannered enough, but it was no secret how fierce she could be when provoked to anger. Zeus no doubt wanted to avoid her wrath for not

44

having sought her counsel on the matter of their daughter's marriage.

Hades' chest tightened. He had come here with the intention of moving past any ill will toward Demeter. He had planned to ask for her blessing as well, before he left Olympus, but seeing even Zeus hem at including the overprotective goddess, he knew he could not pay the price if she refused.

His union with Persephone would be blessed by Zeus, and that would have to be enough for Persephone. She must be his queen at all cost, and he would do anything to see that it happened, including leaving Demeter out of the matter on purpose. And if it meant not divulging that information to Persephone...

"Do you not have the final say, brother?" he questioned, stoking the banked embers of his brother's pride and bringing them to life.

"Yes, yes, of course. Take Persephone as your bride."

Hades nodded, satisfied with the outcome of his visit. "Thank you, brother. Your promise has been kept, and I am grateful."

Yet, even as the sweat on his brow dried in the cool mountain air, he could not say all that he felt. He should be elated, overcome with joy and rushing back to his love as quickly as the last vestiges of the sun sank beneath the horizon.

He should be feeling anything but the knot in his stomach twisting tighter.

CHAPTER 7

PERSEPHONE DECIDED TO spend her last day as a maiden in the meadow with her nymphs. Not one of them knew she would soon be a queen, nor did she give away what the smile playing at the corners of her mouth the day long had meant; in what riches—and pleasures—she would soon partake.

Neither had she felt the need to say goodbye to her mother that evening before heading down the mountain to the stream. She would see her again, surely. Hades had professed his love, asked for her hand with the utmost patience and respect, and her mother had seen the good in him. Demeter would know he would be true to his word, which was to honor and cherish her daughter forever, and she would rejoice with Persephone in her happiness.

Besides, Persephone had promised not to utter a word of the proposal, for Hades had asked her not to tell a soul. The secret should be theirs to keep. He'd had that look in his eyes before he'd murmured the words into her neck between soft kisses, and his cheeks had flushed when she'd drawn back to look him in his pleading eyes.

How could she have refused a god like Hades anything? So handsome, so mysterious... so dark and dangerous. The memory of his gaze, the way it swept over her as she'd nodded her answer, drinking her in as if he were the thirstiest of desert sand, made her heart race as she waited beneath the moon for her dark king to arrive.

After some time, however, Persephone's lids grew heavy. If she were to guess, dawn would be approaching soon. Yet, she forced her eyes to remain open, so Hades would not find her asleep in the dark wood.

The fox had come to wait with her and sat beside her quietly; a red sentinel on duty. Every so often, he reached his muzzle forward to sniff the air. It made her realize she had been craning her own neck, straining to hear Hades' approach.

But the arrival of darkness makes no sound.

Patience, Persephone. He will come.

She sighed, relaxing her shoulders. With a wave of her hand, lily of the valley sprang up from the ground, carpeting the forest floor beneath her. The tiny flowers burst open until an infinite expanse of white bells shivered and twinkled under the moonlight, mirroring their celestial counterparts in the night sky.

When the fragrance reached her nostrils, she inhaled, taking in the sweet scent as she stretched the muscles of her neck. Perhaps she could close her eyes, just for a while. What could it hurt? Her red sentinel would wake her if Hades came while she slumbered.

Persephone lay down among the flowers and closed her eyes. Soon she would be in the arms of Hades, but until then, she would rest her head on a fragrant pillow of spring.

Persephone awoke to the sound of bird chatter. She pushed herself up, blinking and disoriented. After surveying the sparkling dew drops on the leaves around her, she squinted up at Helios.

"Hades did not come?" she asked the sun god.

He did not answer and, of course, she knew he would not. Helios never spoke when he took the form of the sun in the sky, only looked down from the heavens as he watched over them. She doubted he could even hear her.

The fox must have left at dawn, scurrying to its den once the sun had risen. She got to her feet, the now frantic chirping putting a finer point on the fact Hades had left her to wonder where he had gone.

What should she do now? She could go to him, but she had no idea where the entrance to Hades' realm was. There were rumors it was an unassuming cave nestled high above in a towering gray mountain, where a waterfall black as night spilled forth from its mouth.

Her belly swirled, and she pressed on it in an attempt to stop the looping. Perhaps he had thought better of making her his queen. Although, she could not think of anything she had done to upset him.

Persephone rose to her feet and began to walk, to where she did not know. She only knew she needed to move, lest the panic smoldering within catch fire and consume her.

He will come, she told herself as she wandered through the trees. She must have patience, for he was a king, with subjects that needed ruling. Perhaps he was ensnared in his own duty.

She thought of those subjects as she picked blackberries to break her fast. Were the souls of the dead mournful and silent? Or was the Underworld fraught with chaos, with the spirits of those crossed over before their time screaming at the injustice?

Persephone would bring them comfort, with whatever light she could bring with her, so they may rest in peace.

What of those evildoers who wreaked havoc while walking upon the Earth, who deserved much and more pain and suffering they inflicted upon their brethren?

She would leave that to Hades.

Her throat swelled at the thought. Her ponderous and tender-hearted Hades. Left to dole out the unsavory task of punishment Zeus did not want. It was no wonder his reputation as a murderous and merciless god preceded him, hiding the truth in the darkest of shadows.

She would do all in her power to illuminate her beloved's true nature.

Persephone pulled the crisp morning air into her lungs as she ate the last of the berries. After licking the sweet juice from her lips, she headed toward the meadow she would miss. She would bless the world above with as many blooms as she could before Hades came for her.

CHAPTER 8

Hades sat in a great winged chair and stared into the flames that raged in the stone hearth, entranced, seeing everything and nothing at once.

He was the brother of Zeus, king over an entire domain, and feared by many, yet he had not been able to face the goddess Demeter. His penchant for rumination, over others and what they thought of him—whether he was worthy of his status as a king—had, once again, cost him greatly. Demeter would have challenged him, denied him his request. He had no doubt his irritation would have caused him to do something that would lend credence to the reputation that preceded him.

And so, he had not gone to meet Persephone as promised. She deserved a husband whom her mother did not despise.

Now here he sat, needing his sweet Persephone, like the tender shoots beneath the dark ground needing the light to thrive.

He had been resolute in his decision until he'd peered into the inky waters of his gazing pool. Surely, the golden-haired beauty of spring would have already forgotten the dark and desolate king of misery. The thought gave him solace but for a moment, for his comfort had been fleeting. He had seen in the water evidence of something otherwise. The crease of her brow, the downturn of her lips, the rejection swimming in her sky-blue eyes as she wandered the meadow calling for him.

Thus, the spark of altruism had caught and was now a raging fire of regret and self-loathing.

His gaze cut to a black mist formed in the chair adjacent to his. He watched as it turned into a shadowy fog, until Hecate took shape, with smooth alabaster skin in stark contrast to her dark cerulean eyes.

"*Khaíre*, Eubulus."

Hades pushed a burst of humorless air through his aquiline nose. The evening was far from good. He sat brooding in front of a fire so intense it rivaled the likes of Hephaestus's forge. His skin would have melted off his bones had he been anything but immortal.

Hades turned his head back toward the inferno. The witch knew full well he did not find the evening *good*.

"You address me as Eubulus," he replied flatly, "knowing I am in no position to give good counsel, that I am, in fact, in desperate need of it."

It was Hecate's turn to bristle.

"I shall take my leave, then," she said, the fog beginning to swirl around her feet.

Hades would not beg the witch to stay, yet he did not want her to leave. He needed guidance in the matter of what to do next. Living without Persephone was impossible.

"I fear I've made a mistake," he murmured.

"Then go to her," Hecate stated bluntly, already knowing the matter of which he spoke.

As if it could be so easily remedied.

"I cannot," he said. "I have not done as promised."

"You are the brother of Zeus. He has given his blessing. Do you truly need any other permission to make Persephone your bride?"

"That is exactly why I *must,* Hecate, don't you see? I am nothing like my philandering brother, to whom my transgressions the gods and goddesses turn a blind eye. I do not take what I want by trickery or by force, nor will I start now."

"Hera does not turn a blind eye. She sees all her husband does with striking clarity," replied Hecate.

"Furthering my point. Goddesses do not forgive... or forget. Ask the countless women who have perished or suffered at the hands of my brother's carnal desires, including our own sisters. You know how tenuous the thread between Demeter and Zeus remains. Do you believe she would willingly agree to a marriage between her most cherished possession and I, one of three notorious brothers of Olympus? Did Athena take her anger out on Poseidon when he ravished her most devout priestess? No, she turned Medusa into a gorgon, with a gaze that turned all to stone, punishing her to a life of terrible solitude and loneliness. Demeter is not as artful as that, I'm afraid. She would not—could not—take her anger out on me. No, she will most certainly take it out on Persephone."

Hecate inhaled deeply, remaining silent as she considered his words. He took this as an invitation to continue.

"I am an outcast, Hecate. The Olympians, save perhaps Hermes, would not side with me in a power struggle with Demeter. Persephone cannot foresee the petty tit for tat that would ensue. Moreover, Persephone does not understand what she would be giving up."

"And what is that?"

"Family," said Hades. "I was never truly accepted by mine. It would be no loss to me, but to Persephone, who is loved and revered by all beyond measure, she would lose..." Hades dropped his head into his hands. "Everything."

"How do you know she wants to keep it? Have you been to the Oracle of Delphi? Has the Pythia spoken as such?"

"You open my wounds further, Hecate."

"Forgive me. I aim only to illuminate the lengths you will go to punish yourself, so that you may see the truth. If you believe you are not worthy, then you are not. Do you love her? Will you honor and cherish her?"

"I would, of that there is no doubt. I have never loved another as much as I love Persephone."

"Then make her your queen. Let them think what they will. There will be no love for you either way."

Hades shook his head, his heart pounding in his chest. "She will find another. She must."

"You have seen with your own eyes that she will not. Your heart is true, Hades. Show her by giving her the chance to choose. Let her decide what she is willing to lose to gain true love."

Just then, as if to give further credence to the witch's words, Persephone's tormented voice echoed from the fountain that held the water of knowing. *Oh Hades... Where are you, my love? Why have you not come for me?*

Hades gripped the granite rim, peering down into the dark crystalline water to see Persephone wandering the meadow. The confusion on her face was more than he could bear, causing any notion of being the noble groom to flee from his mind.

Hades said nothing as he hurried out of the throne room. With a wave of his hand, his golden chariot appeared in the courtyard, inlaid with polished onyx, gleaming even in the perpetual twilight of his domain.

He climbed in with purpose and snatched the leather whip hanging at the front guard. After cracking the heavy air in half, the fog split, billowing to either side as four great stallions, crimson eyes and sleek coats black as the river Styx, took shape within the harnesses. Orphnaeus unleased a hellish scream as the palace gates swung open. His brothers, Aethon, Nyctaeus, and Alastor, reared in response, and with another lash of Hades' whip, they all sprang forward.

CHAPTER 9

PERSEPHONE FELT THE weight of her mother's stare resting upon the crown of her silky golden waves. She dared not look up, instead focusing on the sweet breads drizzled with honey and luscious, ripe fruit laid out before her while they broke their fast.

They dwelled in one of the twelve villas on the mountain, one reserved for each of the Olympians. Zeus's, of course, was the largest and most opulent. Demeter's expansive and open-aired residence was constructed of glittering granite and polished marble. Finely appointed, but not overly done, which suited the austere goddess perfectly. Had Persephone had a say, she thought their surroundings could have been a bit more comfortable, with rugs and cushioned couches, more braziers burning about the space and an abundance of vases filled with fragrant flowers. She certainly wouldn't have chosen such stark surroundings, beautiful though they were in their own way. Her mother was an Olympian, and Persephone the daughter of one of the most powerful goddesses. Why should they live like the Achaeans of Sparta?

Despite Persephone's resolve to ignore her mother's gaze, her cheeks flushed, as if Helios had betrayed her with a kiss of pink from his scorching rays of high noon.

"Is there something vexing you, Kore?" asked Demeter. "You've been anxious these past few days."

"No, mother. I only grow impatient for my marriage."

Persephone did not understand why Hades had not come for her on the day he had promised. Once Demeter had given her blessing, Persephone would have thought her love would have been eager to retrieve her. He must have had his reasons. She had no doubt she would eventually learn, in time, what had delayed her love.

"I see," replied Demeter, her brow arching only the slightest bit. "I suppose it *is* time for you to marry. Is that what you desire, Persephone? To marry?"

"Yes," replied Persephone, a bit breathlessly. A tentative smile tipped her lips upward as she nodded her head. She did not know what had transpired between Hades and Demeter, exactly what words had been

59

exchanged, but if she knew her mother at all, they had come with a stern warning.

Perhaps that was why Hades had not come for her yet?

"Do you know when..." began Persephone.

"When the time is right," finished Demeter. "And not a minute before."

Persephone's smile dropped, along with the hope that her mother had the capacity to be happy that her daughter had found true love.

She controls even this.

She rose from the reclining couch, any appetite she'd had gone. "Please excuse me, mother. I'd like to go to the meadow for a while."

"Yes. Go to the meadow and clear your mind, my child. Marriage is a serious matter. Think on it, for it should be carefully considered."

My child. The words echoed over and again in Persephone's mind.

"I am not a child," she murmured aloud, to the tiny birds perched on the thin branches of a mulberry bush as she passed by on her way to the meadow. "I am her daughter, but I am not a *child.*"

Guilt stabbed at her insides, even as her jaw tightened. She was being insolent, she knew, but exactly how old would she have to be before her mother loosened her grip. Persephone was a goddess, too, after all. A powerful one.

Or was she? Perhaps not, for even though she could make budded blossoms unfurl and tender shoots grow, it seemed she could not open her mother's eyes or expand her mind.

Nor change it.

"Oh, Hades," she cried, overwhelmed and unable to stop her lament. "Where are you, my love? Why have you not come for me?"

Persephone gasped, feeling the rumbling of the earth before she heard the splitting of it. The moment it shook her being, the second it filled her ears, she knew Hades had heard her this time. Tears of relief sprung into her eyes. She could not contain her joy, nor did she want to. Hades had finally come for her.

She heard the cracking of roots and falling of trees as the ground gave way behind her. She turned to see Hades' coal-black horses emerge, each shining coat unmarred by dirt and debris. Clumps of sod flew from beneath equine hooves, torn up and flung out from the force and speed of their powerful gait as they pulled a gleaming golden chariot from the earth.

In it stood Hades, his onyx eyes fixed on her.

As the spot where she stood mounded upward, she rose with it, and when she reached the very top of the cresting earth, Hades reached for her as he rode by in his chariot, a smile ghosting his lips.

He lifted her with ease and pulled her to him, gently setting her down beside him.

He looked down at her, his eyes shining with happiness, and smiled tenderly as he placed a protective arm around her.

But his smile faded when he saw the wet tracks streaming down her face.

His brow furrowed. "My love, why do you cry?"

Persephone took his face in her hands, smoothing the creases away with her thumbs. Her mother was wrong. She did not need to carefully consider anything.

"Because I am happy," she said before crushing her lips to his.

CHAPTER 10

THE EARTH BEHIND Hades closed, knitting itself back together at the same time the ground ahead of him opened. The four horses dove for the split. Hades had no need to crack his whip, for Orphnaeus and Aethon, the swiftest of the four, did not need coaxing to return to the dark depths of the Underworld.

Persephone clung to him, trembling and gripping his hand tightly as his stallions dragged them down into the earth, then further still into jagged darkness. Hades was accustomed to the speed and force with which the horses pulled his chariot, as he was to the sensation of falling when crossing the threshold of the Underworld.

But Persephone was not.

He bent, hovering his mouth close to her ear and whispered, "Hold on tight."

A tiny squeak escaped Persephone's lips at the sudden drop a moment later.

The horses connected with solid ground, the transition so smooth and natural the chariot scarcely pitched at all.

"Your steadfast golden chariot!" exclaimed Persephone, clearly thrilled. "Such beautiful and powerful beasts you command! I've never seen such cohesive power in all my immortal life. Oh, Hades! What other wonders await me?"

Home, Hades wanted to say. *Home awaits you.*

Instead, he allowed his mirth to show in the form of a playful grin. "Wait until you lay eyes on the guardian of my gates, Cerberus. Powerful, yes, but beautiful? You shall have to decide that for yourself."

Fog swirled around them, light from a violet-colored moon illuminating the horses' necks and long, flowing manes as they raced along the shore of the Lethe, the river of forgetting. The loud pounding of their hooves was muffled only slightly by the black sand.

Hades breathed in the hot and humid air of eternal night. Had he ever felt so content? Had his future ever been filled with so much promise? He exhaled a heavy sigh, his elation short-lived.

Was their future full of promise or torment?

He would tell Persephone her mother had not consented to their marriage one day soon, but not now. These first moments with her were too precious. He wanted the memories of them to remain unmarred.

Persephone scattered his thoughts when she looked up at him with a smile. It was—*she* was—as radiant as Helios, even in the hazy purple light. "I cannot wait to make his acquaintance, then."

"You will not have to wait long." Hades gestured toward his shining obsidian palace, looming in the distance.

The River Phlegethon provided a fiery backdrop to the massive structure, creating an imposing sight. He wondered if she found its many spires, tinged blood red from the burning water that filled the moat surrounding his home, beautiful or terrifying.

Before long, the horses skidded to a stop in front of a set of massive wrought iron gates, stomping their hooves with impatience as Hades helped Persephone out of the chariot. Sleek and breathtaking though they were, they were four of the most temperamental beasts residing in his realm, always keen on receiving proper recognition for their service.

"Thank you, dark brothers. Go now, return to your wild abandon until I call upon you next."

Alastor responded to their king with a feral neigh, Nycteus then trumpeting their departure as the beasts bucked and jumped out of their harnesses before tearing off into the darkness. With a wave of his hand, Hades sent his chariot back into the ether, until he had need of it again.

He peered down at Persephone, who took in her surroundings open-mouthed and wide-eyed. He could not begin to guess her thoughts, and it made his insides roil as fiercely as the fiery water of Phlegethon. He could scarcely believe the goddess of spring was standing next to him, let alone there in his realm of gloom, and of her own choosing.

How much time did he have before so much misery and death changed that?

The growl began as a low rumble, gathering in intensity once all three heads of his guardian joined in the deadly chorus.

"Cerberus," Hades called out. "It is your master and king."

Persephone gasped when the towering three-headed beast emerged from the shadows and passed through the iron bars of the gate as if it were a shade.

All three of Cerberus's heads snapped viciously when the monstrous canine spied Persephone. She tried stifling a cry of terror but failed.

"Mighty Cerberus, you are in the presence of the benevolent Persephone, daughter of Olympus, goddess of spring, and soon to be your queen," said Hades with authority.

The guardian stopped its advance. No longer suspicious, it turned its three heads toward Hades, flattened all ears, and submitted with a bow.

Persephone stepped forward, reaching out her hand to touch one of the guardian's heads. Hades caught her by the elbow.

"Perhaps in time, but I do not advise so bold a gesture currently."

Persephone's cheeks flushed a delicate pink. "Yes, of course. I did not mean to offend."

"No offense taken," he replied. He knew this to be true, for the gates swung open of their own accord as Cerberus turned and led the way into the palace grounds. "Come, let me show you around."

Hades took Persephone's hand, leading her along a stone path of granite veined with gold. Hades had never thought much of the rocky ground on either side of the path.

Until now.

"I'm afraid it is now I who offends..." began Hades, his apology for the desolate landscape dying on the vine when Persephone stepped off the path.

He followed her, wondering what she could possibly want to have a closer look at when she suddenly knelt and laid her hand on the barren soil. To Hades' amazement, and utter delight, glowing Moonflowers and fragrant Tuberose sprang from the ground to bloom in the darkness.

She beamed up at him before standing once more and admiring her work. "I hope you don't mind," she said as she brushed the dirt from her hands. "I wanted to see if I could light up the night as well as the day."

"I don't mind at all. In fact, I was on the verge of apologizing for the lack of..." Hades faltered, once again unsure how it was possible that Persephone could want to be *here*, with *him*. "The lack of beauty in this place."

Persephone reached out and caressed his jaw, loosening the tightness that had settled there. Much like the fallow soil yielded new growth when she had infused her power within it, so did her magic make Hades' heart grow full to bursting.

"This place is your kingdom, and though it is dark, it is wonderous, with many beautiful things hidden within. Your realm is but a reflection of you, Hades, and I am quite in love with it."

Sensing his happiness, a pack of wolves howled in the distance as he drew Persephone to him for a kiss.

Hades nearly groaned when he felt the eddies of air swirling behind him. Of course, the witch would deem this tenderest of moments to be the perfect time for an introduction.

CHAPTER 11

PERSEPHONE'S GAZE WENT from Hades to the tendril of mist that rose from the ground behind him. He turned, and they both watched as a dark figure began to take form.

Once the funnel of smoke had cleared, Persephone could not help but inhale sharply at the woman standing there, for she appeared ghostly. Dark circles bled down from her vacant eyes, haunting the hollows of her cheeks, and her pale skin said little of vitality.

Yet, there this mysterious specter stood, as solid in flesh and alive in spirit as Persephone herself.

"I presume you have heard of the goddess of shades," began Hades. "...of graves and..."

"Sorcery and crossroads," finished Persephone, the knowledge of who stood before them dawning on her immediately. "Yes, I have heard. It is an honor to stand in your presence, Hecate."

The dark goddess nodded, a whisper of a smile ghosting her lips, as though she were a cat toying with a mouse. Persephone wondered if the goddess had sensed her apprehension, even though she had done her best to keep her voice steady. Or was she pleased Persephone had not shied away in fear?

True to her nature, she longed to reach out and touch Hecate, to bring light where there seemed very little, but she refrained. It was clear by the look on her face Hecate did no dealings in light, only shadow.

As if the goddess of witches knew what she had been thinking, she tilted her head, quick and halting, like that of a keen-eyed raven. "And I have heard much and more about you, Persephone," she rasped, the sound of her voice more airy than unpleasant. "The great king of the Underworld is enamored with you, and I can see why."

Entranced, Persephone couldn't help but notice how the witch's words, once spoken, dissipated like smoke. She knew Hecate's countenance, from her grim appearance to her eerie voice, was meant to unnerve her. What the witch had not anticipated, however, was that Persephone was not afraid of the dark. It was inextricably intertwined with the light, for without one the other could not exist, and neither was more malevolent—or benevolent—than the other.

"And I with him. I am to be his queen," replied Persephone.

"Such wonderful news." The fabric of Hecate's skirts billowed, even though there was no wind. She arched one brow, her head moving again in that strange birdlike manner. "Does Demeter prepare to travel to the Underworld to see her daughter avow herself to the king of the Underworld?"

Persephone heard the small intake of breath from Hades, causing her gaze to shift just in time to see something flash in his narrowed eyes. Irritation?

Hecate's inquiry had been meant for Persephone, but it was Hades who answered. "Demeter will not be coming to the Underworld." His words bore an edge Persephone had never heard before.

She turned toward Hades with a furrowed brow. "Why not? I thought you—"

"My love, none of the Olympians are permitted into my domain," he said quickly. "Only the psychopomp Hermes has been granted the ability to traverse between above and below."

"But surely she—"

"Not unless they are given permission by its ruler, of course," interrupted Hecate. "I'm sure in your haste to reunite with the fair Persephone, it slipped your mind to extend an invitation. I am quite sure Demeter would move heaven and earth to attend the *sudden* betrothal of her daughter." She lifted both brows while saying this, pointing a look at him Persephone did not miss. "It would be my pleasure to extend the invitation to Demeter in your stead, Hades."

Persephone bit the inside of her lip, Hecate's emphasis on the word *sudden* did not set well with her. Her mother knew about the marriage, did she not? They had discussed it just this morning.

Hecate's words held another meaning, Persephone was sure of it. What, she did not know. Although her departure had been sudden, surely it had been expected? Even more puzzling now that she thought about it, and perhaps she had been too wrapped up in the anticipation, but her mother had not mentioned she would not be permitted to attend the wedding. Persephone thought it odd her mother would acquiesce to this so easily.

Further proof she only thinks of herself and her happiness.

Hades stared at Hecate, unblinking. Persephone could not read his expression, but the tension between them was palpable, and it made the steady beat of her heart falter. Had they been lovers before Hades and Persephone met? Were they still? Had Hecate been the reason why it had taken Hades so long to come for her?

Was her mother correct? Were all men, even gods, lustful and dishonest?

Instead of screaming, Persephone willed her racing thoughts to slow, calling them into order so she might think with her head and not her heart. Her heart had led her to this place, and she was grateful, but to stay here, she must now employ her wits.

As much as it would devastate her if Hades' love turned out to be false, Persephone could not let the opportunity to be the ruler of her own life pass her by. She loved Hades, enough to forgive him for any lovers he had taken in the past, or may take in the future, although she did not think he would. He was hers now, in heart, soul, and soon to be body, of this she had no doubt.

"Yes," said Persephone. "Please do extend an invitation to Demeter. My marriage would not be the same without her attendance." She turned toward Hades and threaded her arm through his. "Shall we continue on, my love?"

Hades and Hecate exchanged another look. It went on a beat too long, and Persephone gently cleared her throat, indicating that whatever was going on between them was no longer of consequence and should come to an end.

"Yes, of course. I will show you around my—*our*—palace," replied Hades. He took her hand in his and squeezed. Persephone had little doubt he was affirming what had once been, if anything, between him and the witch should be of little concern to her.

She appreciated it, truly, but she would continue to keep her guard up. If having an overbearing mother had taught her anything, it was that she must be vigilant.

"Afterward, let us waste no more time in announcing to the loyal subjects of the Underworld their king is to take a queen," said Persephone.

Now that she was free from her mother's authority, she was determined to exercise hers. She would show her mother that she, Persephone, warm and welcoming goddess of spring, would be in control of her own destiny from this point onward, and her decision was final.

"The denizens will also want a grand celebration, will they not?" rasped Hecate.

Persephone tilted her head at the witch. Where Persephone had referred to them as subjects, Hecate had called them denizens. The distinction niggled at her. Persephone had not intended to be unkind.

"I think that is a lovely idea" she replied, reminded that her newfound personal power must not go to her head. "How about you, Hades? Do you think it a lovely idea?"

"Of course." He nodded in agreement, but his smile was tight.

Persephone's mind raced again as they continued down the path that led to the palace door. This entire exchange between the three of them held an air of something she could not quite grasp. Was it jealousy? Had her arrival upset some sort of delicate balance of power the witch thought she had?

Though Hecate's call for a celebration had been welcomed, Persephone could not distinguish whether it had been born of genuine happiness, or if it had been a thinly veiled challenge for Hades' favor—and those he presided over.

Persephone thought for a moment longer before deciding that, although Hecate may have possessed his favor previously, it was now hers, for Hades had chosen her to be his bride. And she was truly excited to have it all—the man, the marriage, and the freedom.

No longer would she be the naïve maiden longing for love, uncertain about her future and her place among goddesses.

CHAPTER 12

HADES FELT THE magic ignite in Persephone's fingertips as they skimmed down his arm. When she sprang ahead to sprinkle the palace courtyard with narcissus flowers of deep red, Hades silently thanked the Fates for giving him this opportunity to address the witch's ludicrous suggestion to present Demeter with a wedding invitation.

It was more than ludicrous. It was reckless and dangerous. Her presence was what needed to be avoided, at all costs, not encouraged.

His nostrils flared when he rounded on Hecate, who had been following closely behind he and Persephone as they continued down the path.

"Are you mad, witch?"

Hecate narrowed her eyes before vanishing. He knew she had reappeared behind him, for it would be like the goddess to do so.

"Are you daft, king?"

Hades closed his eyes and, lips pressed thin, drew in a breath. He turned around, exhaling as he set his sights on Hecate, who had kept walking. He glanced at Persephone, who was still calling forth blooms, and quickened his pace, grateful she hadn't seemed to notice anything was amiss.

Now beside Hecate, he stared ahead as he spoke, careful not to raise suspicion should Persephone see them out of the corner of her beautiful and very perceptive eyes. "An invitation?"

"Yes," replied Hecate. "I offered to be the bearer of good news, that is all. It does not mean the invitation will be extended, especially if the goddess of the grain harvest is not open to receiving one. My sources tell me she frantically searches as we speak. You are not well liked, Hades, and even though I am a friend to you, many are not."

Hades ground his teeth. Why must Hecate remind him of this. And why did she insist on making him work so hard to puzzle out every word she spoke? This was no time for deciphering riddles.

"I do not follow. Make your meaning plain."

Hecate sighed, clearly disappointed he did not understand whatever plan she was devising. "We kill two birds with one stone."

We? Since when would Hecate suffer the consequences of his rash decision? He alone would be the one to pay for his mistake, not her.

"It is a way for me to see what Demeter knows, and how close to your doorstep she treads." She paused, giving her words time to sink in. Hades nodded, beginning to see the plan within them take shape. He obviously could not speak with Demeter now—that ship had sailed—without revealing to Persephone he had done only half of what he had promised to do.

Hecate continued, "If I am able to convince the goddess that her daughter is safe, sound, and absent of her own accord, perhaps a clash of wills can be avoided."

Hades resisted the urge to rake his fingers through his hair. It was doubtful Demeter could be convinced of anything, but Hecate was right. There were some very strong wills involved at this point, including, as it turned out, Persephone's. She had made it clear she would no longer be accommodating anyone. Not her mother, not the witch, and most certainly not him.

He knew Demeter would not take this burgeoning version of her daughter lying down. The goddess of the harvest was an Olympian, one of the elite deities who were unaccustomed to defiance of any sort. They expected obedience. Believed they were entitled to it.

Demeter was no different, and Hades had no doubt she would do whatever it took to have the compliance she demanded.

"And what if she accepts my invitation only to gain access to my domain? So that she can take Persephone back by force? What would I do then? If I allow Demeter through my gates and lose my one true love because of it, would my misery be anyone's fault but my own?"

"Then you must have assurance Persephone is no longer hers to take."

Hades swallowed hard. It was a true enough statement, but what assurance did any of them have when it came to the affairs of the gods? He loved Persephone, and she him, but he also knew of the loyalty she felt towards her mother, and how the two warred for dominance within her.

The question of Demeter finding her daughter was not if, but when. She would not rest until she had done so. Trickery was not uncommon among his brethren. The gods and goddesses of Olympus used it all the time to get what they wanted. Demeter would not be above feigning happiness to gain access into the Underworld.

On the other side of it, if he forbade Hecate to extend an invitation, how would he explain when the guest of honor's chair sat empty? Persephone would think Demeter uncaring, and her heart would be crushed. The love of his life would be tormented by this, and most certainly wind up going to Olympus to learn the reason why, for she was proving to be as strong-willed as her mother.

A will of her own. One of the many things he loved about her.

As rash and without foresight as it had been, Hades had made his decision to exclude Demeter. Guilt tore at his insides, the err of his ways abundantly clear. He truly amounted to nothing more than a coward. It was an echo of the past that would not stop resounding. He needed to be saved again, and he had no choice but to rely on Persephone to do what he could not.

The flames in the hearth danced around logs of Cypress wood, filling the air with the fragrance of the forest: rich earth, moss, and evergreen. Tall trees ringed the space, their shape barely visible in the dark. Above them, Hades had glamoured the ceiling to look as though it were the night sky, complete with twinkling stars. Tall grass swayed silently in a soundless wind as they laid in the middle of a meadow—her meadow—upon rugs of fur and pillows of fine silk and linen. Instead of sun-loving butterflies, giant glowing Luna Moths fluttered their wings. He didn't think Persephone would mind the change.

Hades lay on his side, with his head propped up on one hand, Persephone on her back, hair splayed around her as she gazed up at the stars. Bottles of wine sat atop low stools, all within easy reach. He had wanted to make her first night in the palace special, going so far as to recreate the stream where they had met under the cover of night. The water trickled over the stones soothingly as they laid there, and judging by her sighs of contentment, he had succeeded in creating the perfect setting to enjoy each other's company for the evening.

"This is lovely. Thank you."

She wore no crown, not yet, but the mulberry silk draped over her lovely form and pinned in place with ornately crafted brooches made her look regal beyond compare. She didn't need a crown to be a queen, no, but come morning, the most precious metals and sparkling gems would sit atop her head, leaving no doubt to all who saw her.

"Is this a dream?" said Hades, caressing Persephone's arm.

Persephone laughed, and he grinned at the smooth sound that fell from her lips, softer than rose petals.

"If it is, then do not wake me!"

He laughed, too, stroking her head.

"I cannot wait for our wedding tomorrow," he began, running his fingers through the unbound waves. "But I wonder if a *grand* celebration is necessary. Perhaps we have a private ceremony and then go on tour, visiting each land within our realm individually?"

He wasn't suggesting the celebration should be skipped all together, necessarily, but if she agreed to forgo a gathering at the palace, he would not object. Knowing the gods and goddesses of Olympus, that would be the time and place Demeter would come crashing in to ruin the happiness they'd found, for they were purveyors of dark irony. Moreover, the dressing down that would be sure to follow would be witnessed by nearly every soul that inhabited his realm.

"We could, if that is what you desire, but what of our guests? Would we leave them so abruptly?" said Persephone.

Hades knew she was referring to Demeter. It was possible she hoped Zeus might make an appearance as well.

"You're right," he replied, deciding not to press the matter further. "The Olympians take offense easily."

"Is that why I have never seen you among the frivolity atop the mountain?" she said, rolling toward him.

He caressed her bare shoulder. "My darling, frivolity has never been my way, and as you have learned, I prefer the privacy and comfort of my dark domain." He shifted closer, leaning down and kissing her. "Besides, I have never been invited."

Persephone frowned, which he hadn't intended to make her do.

Hades leaned back, easing onto his back and pulling her with him. "Come now, don't let it vex you. You know I could never live in that world, even if I had wanted to. I spend too much time in my head. I would have made a terrible Olympian."

She laughed, light and airy, as was her way. "Well, I, for one, think you would have made an excellent Olympian."

"And why is that?" he asked, genuinely curious.

"Why, your reputation proceeds you," she replied, "and isn't that the half of what makes them so feared?"

Hades feigned an incredulous look. He wasn't serious, of course, but it gave him an excuse to pin her beneath him in mock indignation.

"How dare you insult me, goddess," he said, loosely caging her shoulders between his forearms.

She reached up, and his heart stuttered when she traced a thumb over his lips. "Have I offended you oh mighty Ruler of the Underworld?" She smiled mischievously.

"You have," he said, arching a brow at her. "And I'm afraid you're going to have to pay the price."

His gaze dropped to her neck, and she lifted her chin in response, offering the arch of her throat to him to accept her punishment. He wasted no time pressing his lips to the supple skin there and delivering it.

She smelled of sweet grass and honey, wildflowers and spring rain. He wanted to devour her, every inch, until her sounds of contentment became moans of pleasure. He would have continued his quest if it hadn't been for the sudden and overwhelming feeling of being watched.

He lifted his head and peered into the darkness. A set of amber eyes, glowing ever so faintly in the night, stared back at him.

"What is it?" whispered Persephone, her fingers still entwined in his hair.

Hades did not answer, but drew himself up, taking her with him and folding his arms around her protectively.

"Show yourself," he called out, wondering if a lost soul had found its way into the palace. It wasn't uncommon for it to happen, and souls weren't dangerous, necessarily, but they couldn't exactly be left to roam aimlessly down his corridors.

He was about to call out again when a fox, the very one from the meadow above, gingerly stepped out of the dark. It walked toward them, head bent low, before sitting and awaiting its fate for trespassing.

Hades sighed, and he felt Persephone's grip on him loosen.

"He likes you," she said, trying to stifle her a laugh as she reached a hand toward the fox. The animal happily obliged, compelled to her as surely as a moth is to a flame.

"And I him," said Hades, grinning.

He kissed her temple before scratching her red sentinel behind its large ears. He knew all

too well the irresistible pull when the fair
Persephone beckoned.

CHAPTER 13

HADES RELEASED THE thick velvet curtains of his personal chambers from their corded tiebacks, letting them fall closed. After their visitor in the meadow, he had asked if she would like to reconvene someplace more private. They had parted only an hour ago, but he could hardly wait to be with her again.

He stood in front of the hearth, trying not to think of the way the silk had clung to her body, leaving nothing to the imagination, and how feverish her skin had turned when he kissed her. It was an impossible task. She ignited in him a lust and longing so strong it was almost unbearable. Truth be told, he almost took her then and there, but he had quickly thought better of it. He would not dream of forcing himself upon her, and so, with smoldering eyes, he invited her to meet him in his room, so they could continue their lively... conversation.

Oh, the way she had blushed.

The reflection in the grand mirror hanging above the mantle stared back at him, scrutinizing his intentions. He, of course, would relish it if the union of their bodies happened this night, but there was another reason he had wanted to keep her close.

Despite the smile on his face that had been present all day, the fear Demeter would find a way into his realm, showing up unannounced and furious, gnawed at him without mercy.

It was true, he wanted to be with Persephone every moment of every day. But it was also true that, as the hours passed, he did not want Persephone to be alone for long stretches of time. There must be no opportunity for Demeter to separate them.

Hades unleashed a sigh, thoroughly amazed at how quickly his emotions could change, from complete happiness to utter longing to unrelenting fear in the blink of an eye. Not so long ago, he had agonized in front of this very same hearth, over whether he possessed the will to live without Persephone. He had quickly found out he did not, and now here he was, her on the verge of being his queen, and him sick over the thought that he may lose her by his own reckless folly.

He shook the thought away, determined to take comfort in knowing that tomorrow morning they would be husband and wife, and sat in the cushioned reading chair next to the fireplace.

Not long after they had arrived that morning, he had made it known that he and a daughter of Olympus were to be wed the next day. From the highest balcony of his obsidian palace, he had announced a celebration would take place tomorrow evening, and all were invited to attend, except those condemned to the pits of Tartarus. The fallen heroes of Elysium had clapped and cheered, raised their spears and swords high, but those who inhabited the meadows of Asphodel had done naught but stare up at his fair Persephone in silence.

He had expected as much from those souls who were left to wander in mindlessness after drinking from the waters of the river Lethe. Their kin may not have had the means to properly lay their loved ones to rest, or they were forbidden from doing so, as was the case with the renowned Trojan warrior Hector. Hades thought it kinder to have them sip from the waters of forgetting so they may at least exist in blissful unawareness instead of never-ending torment.

Hades quietly scoffed at the thought. None of the Olympians had ever bothered to ask why the shades of the underworld wandered with an aimless indifference. Hades supposed they would have realized it was a kindness rather than a punishment, and the gods and goddesses of Olympus would rather cling to the notion that he was cruel than admit their judgment of his character had been not only harsh but wrong.

A log in the fire broke, falling in on itself and sending a spray of sparks shooting upwards. When the fire settled, Hecate appeared in the flames.

"What news have you?" asked Hades, drawing his chair closer to the fire and silently thanking the witch for using a more hidden mode of communication. Persephone, though mild-mannered and gentle, may grow even more suspicious than she already was should she happen upon Hades and the witch in his private chambers. Persephone would come to realize in time that he and Hecate's bond was platonic. Until then, he did not want to give her any more reason to think otherwise.

"There is trouble," replied Hecate. "Demeter frantically searches for her missing daughter."

"And what did you do?"

"I lit a flame in my torch and aided in the search, of course. I thought it best not to give up her daughter's whereabouts until she was less frantic. That time never came, for she beat upon her breast with agony so loud, Helios took pity on her distress and divulged all that he knew."

"Helios?" asked Hades, confused as to what the sun god could possibly have known when it suddenly dawned on him. "He saw everything."

"Yes, and from the sky, it looked as though you had taken her against her will."

"But I did not!" said Hades, exasperated.

"It is no secret you are not well liked, Hades. As such, Helios saw only your actions, not what was in your heart."

"They were tears of joy, Hecate. Words from her own mouth."

"Words spoken only to you. It is unfortunate that Helios only saw what he wanted to see, but he meant well, for he was moved by her suffering. I tried my best to soothe her, but it was no use."

Hades raked a hand through his hair. "What happened next?"

"She fled in the direction of Olympus, vowing there will be no harvest until her daughter has been returned to her."

Hades scrubbed a hand over his face, trying to quiet the screaming inside his head. She would appeal to Zeus, and his mighty brother's part in all of this would undoubtedly be overlooked. "Demeter will be relentless. There is nothing the gods love more than an offering, dripping with fat. Without the harvest, the animals will waste away. My brother will concede."

Hades inhaled deeply before exhaling. What a mess he had created. This was proof he should have done right by Persephone and sought out Demeter as well while on the mountain that day.

Would Demeter have agreed? Hardly, but at least there would be no misinterpretation of his intentions when it came to her daughter. Because Hades had let his pride rule him, Demeter believed Persephone to be kidnapped by the cruel black sheep of the family. Demeter had experienced a panic so immense, and then a rage so blinding, there would be no reasoning with her, even for Persephone. She would make everyone, gods and mortals, suffer.

New ideas began to take shape in Hades' mind, fusing themselves with the thoughts already there. Demeter would come, invitation or not. She had most likely already appealed to Zeus, laying her terms before him. How long would it take before Zeus gave in to them. A week? A day? Within the hour?

It made everything within Hades roil knowing that if Demeter was allowed to enter his domain, she would try to convince Persephone to return to the light of the world above by playing upon the bond between mother and daughter. She may very well succeed, especially once the knowledge that he had been deceptive was revealed.

What might Persephone do when she learned her mother had not been amenable to the marriage? That, in truth, his ego had driven him to not even offer the courtesy of asking. He was confident Persephone loved him, but did she love him enough to forgive him?

He felt in his heart there was a good chance she would stand up to her mother and stay, but there was also a part of him that feared she would not forgive him for lying and leave. She was his reason for existence, and he could not bear to live without her.

"It's only a matter of time before I must face the consequences of what I have done," said Hades.

"Then you must tell her."

"Yes, I have no doubt Demeter will be at my gates imminently. I need to warn Cerberus of her arrival—"

"I mean Persephone," said Hecate. "She is your best defense against Demeter."

"But I have lied by omission. Persephone will leave me."

"Not if she is bound to you, to this world. Seduce her Hades, tonight. Have her taste the food of the Underworld."

He turned to look when the bodiless visage of Hecate nodded at something behind him. On a small table was a bowl of pomegranates.

"I... No, I can't..." he stammered, shaking his head. "I've already been untruthful enough. Why would I hasten her abandonment of me?"

No, nothing good would come of it. He would surely lose Persephone to Demeter, and the only one he would be able to blame was himself.

"The ever-honorable Hades. Giving those who have never fought fairly a day in their existence an easy victory. I say use the reputation they have insisted upon giving you to your advantage—"

A knock sounded on the chamber door, causing Hades' heart to nearly leap from his chest.

In that moment, as selfish as it was, he knew he would do anything, no matter how deceitful, to keep her with him. That included binding her to the Underworld, so that by the law of the gods, she could not leave, for whoever eats the food of his dark realm is bound to stay in it forever.

"That is your counsel?" whispered Hades.

"That is my counsel," Hecate whispered back, vanishing from the flames just as a second knock at the door sounded.

CHAPTER 14

PERSEPHONE'S HEART HAMMERED in anticipation. Having been impatient, she had knocked twice. How was it that she stood at the chamber door of Hades, the ruler of the Underworld, on the eve of their wedding no less? She hoped he didn't think her too eager for his company, though she was, and suspected he knew it.

He had asked her to convalesce in his chambers so that they might enjoy lively... conversation, was it he said? She secretly hoped he meant they would engage in more than that. Finish what it was that had been started in the meadow he had recreated for her, fox and all. He was a god and she a goddess. They were not bound by any morality laws to wait until wedlock to consummate their marriage.

The truth? She could hardly believe all that had transpired. Wasn't it barely a fortnight ago when he had asked her to be his queen? Now here she was, longing to fall into his arms—and into his bed—with little to no talking.

The door swung open, and there stood Hades, wearing a short tunic, draped across one shoulder, putting the fine cut of his broad chest on display. In that moment, when the sultry scent of dusky smoke, sweet incense, and spicy cloves reached her senses, she was sure the jasmine-infused oil she had rubbed through her hair, on her wrists and between her breasts, had been left in the bathing room quite on purpose.

"There you are, my love," said Hades, a dazzling smile playing upon his lips. "Come in."

Did he have the same night in mind as she? It certainly seemed so.

Persephone did her best to glide into the room, though she wasn't sure how well her trembling limbs accomplished the goal. If her unstable gait had not given away her nerves, the firm peaks under the thin silk of her chiton surely gave away her desires.

She walked past him, smiling demurely before taking a seat on one of two cushioned reclining couches. Between them sat a bowl of pomegranates. Persephone had to stifle her satisfaction when Hades cleared his throat, her eyes refusing to leave his lean and muscled form as he took the couch opposite hers.

"I trust you have not changed your mind?" asked Hades, plucking one of the pomegranates out of the large golden bowl.

"Changed my mind about what?" asked Persephone. "Engaging in lively conversation?"

A half smile cocked one of Hades cheeks and Persephone had to force herself not to wilt like a delicate bloom under Helios's too-hot rays.

"I meant about being my queen." His eyes never left hers as he pressed his thumbs into the firm outer flesh of the rosy fruit.

"I have not changed my mind," she replied, a bit breathless but determined to keep her composure. "In fact, what if I told you I have no desire for conversation at present?"

Hades' grin vanished as he split open the fruit, its flesh yielding easily, and he dug his thumbs into it further. Juice burst from the seeds, running down his wrists. He raised his arm and lapped at the sticky liquid until his lips were stained red.

Finally, he licked his lips and said, "Then I would say come to me, Persephone."

Warmth pooled low in her belly, and she rose to her feet as though she were in a trance. Fire surged through her veins at the sight of Hades' juice-stained lips. She found herself standing before him, and when she kneeled, she placed one of his fingers into her mouth so that she could taste the tart flavor of the pomegranate juice as well.

Hades moaned, the evidence of his desire plain, and pulled her into his lap and onto the hard line of him. She sighed at the exquisite ache forming between her thighs as his hand slid under her chiton, deft fingers searching. She arched her back, lifting her hips so that he could find the delicate flesh he sought.

With each stroke, Persephone felt herself grow more feral with lust. Without even knowing what she was doing, she plunged her fingers into the pomegranate, breaking the seeds so more of the juice spilled out. She slipped a finger into Hades' mouth. The sensation drove her wild, and before long she had pulled out more of the luscious seeds. She raised them to her mouth, hardly able to wait for the flood of tart liquid as the seeds burst in her mouth.

CHAPTER 15

HADES WAS SO overpowered by his desire he barely caught her wrist in time. Her fingers instinctively wrapped themselves around the seeds to protect them from falling out of her sticky palm.

"I cannot do this," he murmured, more to himself than her but that did not stop the questions that followed.

"What do you mean you cannot do this?" she asked, worried. "Do you not desire me?"

The stricken look on her face made his heart break wide open. "I do desire you, more than you can imagine. My heart beats for no one else but you. You are my one and only love, Persephone."

Persephone glanced at her closed fist before setting her gaze back on him. "Then what is it you cannot do?"

Her face was flushed with not only desire, but embarrassment, and it made Hades feel even worse. What had he done?

"Let you eat the seeds," replied Hades.

Her brows knitted themselves together at first, but then arched in surprise when he gently pried open her fingers and gave her wrist a slight shake. Confusion deepened the color on her face as she watched the seeds drop to the marble floor.

"Hades?" she said, her sunlight hair falling in soft waves when she tilted her head at him. "What has gotten into you?

He nearly groaned in agony. He did not want to tell her, but he knew he must. He closed his eyes and inhaled. Eager to be rid of the awful secret, he forced his lids open so that he could look Persephone in the eyes. "I have a confession to make."

She blinked, the crimson on her cheeks now creeping down her neck and onto her chest. "You desire me," she began, "but you still wish to take Hecate into your bed. Is that it?"

It was a rhetorical question, and her voice had been so certain it knocked him off balance for a moment. She wholeheartedly believed she knew the reason he had stopped her from eating the seeds was because of greed, that he wanted both her *and* Hecate to satisfy his desires. The notion was ridiculous to him, causing his mouth to go slightly agape.

The emotion rimming her eyes welled into tears, and she tried to move away from him. He grasped her by the shoulders and held her in place. "No, Hecate and I are not lovers. We never have been, nor will we ever be."

She shrugged off his hands. "I saw the looks between the two of you, Hades. Do not deceive me!"

"You're right. I do deceive you." He took hold of her wrists when she tried to pull away once more. "But not about that. Please, Persephone, listen to me." He took her face in his hands, directing her downcast gaze up to meet his. "Hecate is my closest confidant, yes, but gives me nothing but counsel. I swear it."

She relaxed, the anger melting from her face, leaving only confusion. "Then what is the meaning of all this? What is the deception you speak of... and why can I not eat the pomegranate seeds?"

He dropped his hands to rest on her thighs. "You can, but not from here. Not while in the Underworld."

"Why not?"

"Because it would be wrong."

"Hades! I grow tired of these riddles. Speak plain. Why can I not eat those seeds?"

He didn't know whether it would be a maniacal laugh or an anguished cry that would burst from him, but he stifled it just the same. How many times had he been on the verge of madness when Hecate had done this very thing? He suddenly had a newfound appreciation for the art of speaking in riddles and rhymes, spinning clever words so they held double meanings. Only, he was not doing it to be clever. He was doing it to delay the inevitable.

Hades sat upright. He could hesitate no longer, and so he did not mince his next words. "I did not ask Demeter for your hand in marriage, only Zeus."

"How could that be?" Persephone shook her head. "She spoke as if a marriage between us had already been agreed upon."

Hades was just as confused as Persephone, though a part of him was grateful for the distraction. Her preoccupation with who Demeter was speaking of, and not the part where he had kept the truth from her, gave him more time to find his bearings.

"She told me marriage was a serious matter and that I must consider it carefully." She spoke more to herself than him, her mind trying to work out the discrepancy.

"She speaks the truth there," replied Hades thoughtfully. "Marriage is quite a serious—"

"Who was she referring to if not you?"

Hades shook his head, just as baffled as Persephone. "Demeter didn't know we had even met let alone that we were in love. Perhaps she had been arranging your betrothal to another without your knowledge?"

"No," she said, her voice heavy with sadness. "I think perhaps she was only humoring me. And I think she would have done so forever. The only thing she cares about is herself. *My* happiness does not matter."

Her tears fell freely now, and it tore at his heart. Although it tempted him greatly, he could not use Demeter's controlling nature as an excuse for the terrible choice he had made. Demeter's careless treatment of her had finally come into sharp focus for Persephone. The realization that a mother could project her own insecurities onto her child and call it love was devastating enough. He could not rub salt into Persephone's already deep and painful wounds.

He would not add insult to injury by blaming Demeter for his mistake.

"I went to Olympus, I swear it, but I brazenly thought Zeus's leave should be enough. My pride got the best of me. I was thinking only of myself, and I was wrong." He tucked a strand of hair behind her ear before brushing away a tear from her cheek. "Trust me when I say I regret letting you believe that I had also asked your mother when I had not. I am sorry I have deceived you."

He did not know if her silence was a good sign or a bad omen.

"What does all that have to do with the seeds?" she asked, her voice so measured it frightened him a little.

"Demeter demands your return, no doubt appealing to Zeus as we speak. She believes you to have been taken against your will. She does not know of our love, nor our plan to marry. When she does learn of it, that her daughter is consort to the dark and terrible Hades, she will do everything in her power to get you back, including enlisting the Olympians to help her do so."

Persephone laid her forehead upon his chest and began to sob. He cradled her head as she wept. Her breath was hot, and her tears wet upon his skin, as she spoke into his chest. "The seeds, Hades," she murmured. "What is it about the seeds?"

Hades steeled himself with a long exhale before giving away the last bit of security he would have that she would remain here with him forever.

"Anyone who eats the food of the Underworld is bound to both me and my domain. I was going to feed you the seeds to ensure that Demeter would have no recourse should—when—she came for you. Make no mistake, when Zeus has finally had enough of her protesting..."

"Protesting?"

"She leaves the world barren and unfruitful."

Persephone shook her head. "She... she would not do that." Hades remained silent, and a moment later, she unleashed a sob as she sagged into the resignation that, yes, it was possible her mother would be that vindictive.

"Without cattle and sheep fattened by the grain harvest, there would be no sacrifices made to the gods," she said softly, looking at him through red-rimmed eyes.

He nodded. "The Olympians would grow restless, not having been paid proper homage, leaving Zeus to contend with many disgruntled gods and goddesses, for they so love their offerings."

She averted her gaze, but he could see her turning it over in her mind, imagining the desolation as her heart broke not for the gods, but for the mortals. When she finally looked at him, she crumpled again, knowing in her heart Demeter was capable of such cruelty.

Hades held onto her, stroking her back gently. "If you were bound to me, Demeter could demand your return all she liked, but by the laws of the Underworld she could not have it, for you would be mine, Persephone."

She sat up again. "Yours?"

"I'm sorry," apologized Hades. "That did not come out how I intended it. I only meant to say that Demeter would no longer have control over you. If you were bound to me, not only by marriage but by law, you would no longer be hers to take."

"Would you control me then?"

"No. No, of course not. You would be free to come and go as you pleased. At liberty to live how you see fit, as a goddess of your worth should."

He scrubbed a hand over his face. Being in his head had always been a dangerous place to be. His way of thinking seemed noble to him, but it did not always come off as such to others. He hoped all he had confessed, along with all that he professed, had been taken as sincerely as he meant it. He hoped his words did not seem patronizing or self-serving, especially at what was quite possibly the most critical moment of his immortal life.

"Did you only invite me to your room to seduce me? Trick me into eating the seeds?"

Hades shook his head, the hand in her hair moving to cup and caress her tear-stained cheek. "Seduce you, yes. Trick you, no. I have never wanted anyone like I want you. My desire for you is real. But as you have found out, I cannot keep anything from you. I have told you all that is in my mind and in my heart. It will not be long until Demeter comes for you. I needed to act quickly."

Persephone wiped what remained of the tears from her swollen eyes. "Did you think me so weak that I would not stand up to my mother."

"No, Persephone. Not in the slightest. I know the guilt you harbor and the sense of duty that keeps the thread between you unbroken when it comes to your mother. I did not want you to have to choose between me or her. Yes, I resorted to attempting to make the choice for you. But it was wrong, and I knew it was wrong, so I did not go through with it. Please forgive me, my love. I beg of you."

Persephone remained silent for so long that he thought he might go mad. When he could bear her silence no longer, he bowed his head until, finally, she spoke.

"My mother has never once confessed the transgressions she has committed against me, let alone apologized for them. But you, Hades, cannot abide by my mistreatment. You have proven that you will not—cannot—do me wrong, even when you stand to gain that which you desire most—someone who knows you, the real you, and loves you despite what others think. Don't you see, Hades? I am already bound to you. You have given me the freedom to choose what's best for *me*."

Her gaze dropped to her wrists. In his fervor to be forgiven, he had once again grabbed hold. "Let go, and trust in what I choose."

Hades dutifully obeyed. When she leaned over him, he ran his fingertips over her ribs, planting as many reverent kisses on her soft skin, warm and smelling of jasmine, as he could before the moment was over. He didn't know her intent, or what would come next. He only knew he wanted to remain in the moment, suspended in the possibility of forgiveness, and would do so forever if she allowed him to.

When Persephone pulled back to look him in the eyes, she held another pomegranate in her hand. Hades dared not let himself think about what it might mean. But he did hold out hope that whatever it was, it would mean forever.

"I am not my mother's possession."

Hades opened his mouth to agree, but Persephone pressed a finger to his lips.

"Neither am I yours," she said, pushing him back on the couch. "Unless I choose to be." She removed her finger from his lips to place her hand on his chest. "And I, my love, choose to be."

She moved her hips, awakening his lust once again, and whispered against his lips, "Do not try to deceive me ever again."

"Never," he said before claiming her mouth.

She guided him into her, and he matched her movements, which were slow and cautious. He would do everything in his power to take his time with her, giving as much pleasure as he took.

They rolled into each other until soft moans became urgent panting, and Hades held onto her as she moved above him, lost in her softness. Her pale skin flushed with desire as she split open the pomegranate. When she opened her mouth, intending to be fed, Hades understood.

He did not hesitate to oblige her request to secure the fate of her choosing. He plucked out six seeds and placed them between her kiss-swollen lips. She chewed in time with his thrusts. He pressed a kiss to her lips as she took control of her own destiny by swallowing the seeds. When her mouth parted to issue a throaty cry of pleasure, her flaxen hair turned as black as a raven's wing.

It was done. She was bound to him. And of her own accord.

Awed by her transformation from light to dark, he pulled her closer to him and whispered, "My queen," into the hollow of her throat.

CHAPTER 16

WHITE MOONFLOWERS TUCKED into long inky tresses embodied all that Persephone had become. A goddess of light and dark, a queen of both death and rebirth. As she stepped out onto the balcony, Hades knew, beyond a shadow of a doubt, their marriage was fated.

She walked through the arched doorway slowly, looking out over the balcony railing, peering down at all those below who had gathered to witness their king crown his queen. She clutched a small bouquet of black and white anemone, and when Hades noticed the petals shivering slightly, he offered her a reassuring smile when she turned to face him.

She smiled back, the beauty of it rendering him speechless. Furthering his inability to form words, which he would need to do very soon, was what she wore. It was not a dress made of dawn, but of midnight, embroidered and beaded with the deep blues and purples of twilight.

Hecate stood off to the side, holding a satin pillow on which rested a tiara. It matched his own crown, metal forged black in the fiery river of the Underworld set with precious diamonds, both dark and light.

He could barely wait to place it atop her head.

"Persephone," said Hades, taking her hands and drawing her closer to him. "I swear to you my honor, my love, and my loyalty for eternity."

It was all he could manage to get out, but it was enough, for she nodded and repeated the promise back to him through lips tinted blood red. He was so mesmerized by them, and by her cloudless sky-blue eyes, that he barely felt Hecate's looming presence at his back. Reason and clarity hit, however, when she thrust the pillow in front of him.

He reached for it with careful hands, still trying to comprehend the goddess before him would be his queen once he crowned her and sealed their union with a kiss.

Hades stepped closer, looking into her eyes as he placed the symbol of his undying love upon her head.

"My fair queen," he said, glancing at the crowd through the scrolled iron railing before meeting her gaze once again. "Shall we?"

"My dark king," she replied. "We shall."

Hades led her to the edge of the balcony.

"Denizens of the Underworld," he began, his voice ringing out strong and true as he lifted their joined hands. "I present your queen, the fair and just Persephone, goddess of life *and* death."

Hades bent down to kiss his bride, and the roar of the Underworld was deafening the moment his lips met hers.

The merriment lasted nine days, until finally, on the tenth, Hades and Persephone finally dined alone.

She sat across from him, her raven hair shining blue-black in the dim light. Bowls of pomegranates and plates of sugared plums, bread, nuts, and cheeses, along with several goblets of sweet dark wine and gilded vases of fragrant flowers dotted the table between them. He secretly admired the way the jewels in her crown glittered in the candlelight until his smile widened into open appreciation.

He would be a liar, however, if he said there was not some part of him that feared this vibrant dream he was living would soon turn into a dismal nightmare. Demeter had not yet made an appearance, but that did not mean she was not coming. Hades hoped, by some miracle of the Fates, she never would, but he knew that wasn't how the sisters conducted their magic.

Persephone appeared content, but Hades knew all too well the spiral of never-ending worry that swirled in her mind. Neither of them would be at peace until Demeter's attempted coup was over.

He reached for a full goblet. "Be at peace, my love." He took a sip of the wine. "For you are a happily married woman, are you not?"

She smiled. "You know I am. But I suppose now that the celebration is over, it has given my mind room to wander."

Hades set down his cup, nodding in agreement. He knew of what she spoke all too well. Their marriage and the festivities that followed had provided a welcomed distraction. Of course, there had been a chance Demeter might have found a way into the Underworld, but it had been slim. The gods were fickle, but he did not believe Hermes would have agreed to fly Demeter past his gate and to his door. The only other god who could enter the Underworld was Zeus, and Hades did not think he would either, for if he did, the king of the gods would have to admit his part in the goddess of the harvest's grievance.

"We will face what is to come together," said Hades. He went to rise, to go to her, when thunder rumbled in the distance. His gaze cut to Persephone. Her smile faded as she calmly folded her hands in her lap.

It was time. With a wave of his hand, both he and his queen sat upon their shining golden thrones cushioned with silk the color of midnight.

A moment later, the king of the gods appeared in a blinding crack of lightning. Next to him stood Demeter. Hades ground his teeth. He could not help it, for the mere sight of them, knowing the reason they stood in his throne room, prompted him to don his armor, slipping into the role as sinister god of darkness effortlessly.

"Good evening, brother," he said coolly before nodding at Demeter. "Goddess." Not addressing her by name would only add fuel to the fire, and he knew he should show more courtesy than she had shown him, but old habits die hard. "What brings you to the Underworld?"

He silently admonished himself, knowing he should cease his taunting, if not for his sake, then for Persephone's. Further raising the hackles of the Olympian goddess standing before them by feigning ignorance could damage his tenuous alliance with Zeus.

His ever-blunt and always-brazen brother wasted no time, announcing the purpose of their visit without a single pleasantry. "We have come to retrieve the fair... Persephone."

Hades stifled a laugh at Zeus's surprise and Demeter's look of horror at his beloved's change in appearance. He held out his hand to Persephone. She took it, and he squeezed gently.

"Retrieve her?" he asked. "That would imply she had been taken. I believe we had discussed the matter some time ago. Perhaps you meant to say *congratulate* her."

"Congratulate her?" questioned Demeter. "Why would congratulations be in order? You have taken her against her will." The next word she uttered caught in her throat when her gaze landed on Persephone's crown. "No."

Had she not noticed the thrones on which they sat?

"Yes, Demeter," replied Hades. "Your eyes do not deceive you. Persephone is my queen..."

He meant to continue, but the swirling black mist as Hecate began to assemble at the base of the dais caught his eye. Demeter took the opportunity to seize control of the conversation, quickly turning it from civil to hostile.

"Lecherous coward!" she shouted. "You have stolen my daughter and turned her against me with your lies!" She turned on Hecate next, pointing an accusatory finger at her. "And you! Lighting your torches and aiding in the search when you had knowledge of where she was being held captive. I could have stopped this madness had it not been for your treachery, you two-faced witch!"

"Three," stated Hecate, calmly challenging Demeter's vitriol with simple fact.

"My sweet Persephone, what have they done to you?" Demeter did not wait for an answer. She turned toward Zeus, thoroughly enraged and her amber eyes ablaze. "I demand justice! If you are the king of the gods as you say, punish this brazen witch, who has shown where her loyalty lies by conspiring with the dark lord of deceit. Command him to return my daughter to me and let us be done with this."

"Would that he could," mused Hecate aloud, nonplussed and perhaps a bit too delighted by Demeter's rage. "But the fair Persephone has eaten the food of the Underworld, and so he cannot."

A long and suffering sigh emptied Zeus's lungs, indicating to all that he had reached the end of his patience with the matter.

"Is this true?" Zeus immediately pursed his lips, annoyed that the situation had become infinitely more complicated. The problem could no longer be solved by force, which was his preferred method of resolution.

"It is," answered Hades. "She has eaten the seeds of a pomegranate."

"No." Demeter shook her head, her stone façade beginning to crumble. "It cannot be."

Hades knew he should be civil, knew that it was he who owed the goddess the truth, and he would give it, admit that he had been wrong, but he would not apologize for making Persephone his queen.

"And why not? Because your daughter fell in love with *Hades*, the brother whose reputation as the cruel and sinister puppet master of souls is unfounded? You know nothing of me, Demeter. You, so righteous in your conviction, choose to believe me brooding instead of lonely. Refusing to accept that I could have more depth and compassion than the lot of you on Olympus. Instead, you perpetuate the notion that I cruelly condemn the souls of those who enter my domain too soon to a lifetime of madness instead of doing them a kindness by allowing them the bliss of existing only in the current moment. I was wrong not to ask you for Persephone's hand, that much is true, but let your prudish and domineering nature, your narrow-minded rantings and ravings be proof that if I had, you would have denied me the love I so longed for simply because you so vehemently believe I do not deserve it."

"You *are* unworthy! Persephone is pure and you are corrupt. She is my daughter."

"She is also mine," Zeus reminded Demeter, which only made her more venomous.

"How dare you," she spat. "She is the only good thing that came out of it, and she is mine!"

CHAPTER 17

"ENOUGH!" PERSEPHONE SHOUTED with a force rivaling that of her father, surprising even herself when the ground beneath them rumbled. Her gaze shifted between Hades and Zeus before finally settling on Demeter. "Especially you."

Demeter stepped back when Persephone stood, as if she had been pushed. Her hand flew to her chest, over her heart, as though she had been struck.

There was a time not so long ago that such a display would have brought Persephone to heel, but now it only made her more determined.

Persephone squared her shoulders, which now shook from anger and not fear, and leveled a stare at her mother. *Oh, cease this madness, Demeter. Hades is right. The only thing wounded is your pride.*

Come what may between them, her position would be known. She loved Demeter, she always would, but Persephone was a goddess in her own right, and had been kept sheltered under the guise of protection for far too long.

"There seems to be some confusion regarding who I am," said Persephone. "I am the goddess of spring, growth, and rebirth. You may oversee the harvest, Demeter, but it is I who calls forth the rain so that the crops may grow and usher in the warmth so they may thrive."

The set of her mother's jaw grew tighter at the use of her proper name, for Persephone had always played the role of the subordinate child and not the grown equal. A small part of her regretted it, but there was no stopping a tempest once it had begun.

"I am also the Queen of the Underworld, by my own free will. I was not taken by force." She saw Hades tip his chin upward out of the corner of her eye. "And now that I have cleared up any confusion regarding who I am, I shall inform you of who I am not."

This was the moment Persephone had dreaded and longed for all at once.

"I am not a possession," she calmly stated before gesturing to Hades. "Not his." Her gaze narrowed on Demeter, sharp and cutting, as she dropped her arm to her side. "And not yours."

"What happened to you, Kore?" cried Demeter, moving toward Persephone. "You used to be so sweet and helpful, child."

124

Don't you mean accommodating and compliant?

Persephone stood her ground, moved naught an inch by Demeter's flattering words, for pandering compliments no longer played upon her heartstrings.

"I am no longer a maiden," replied Persephone. "I am a goddess and a queen, and you will call me by my name, which is Persephone."

Zeus raised his eyebrows, grabbing a wrist and pressing his lips together to hide his approval at her most brazen proclamation. It was obvious he saw himself in her and was quite pleased.

"No," pleaded Demeter, her hands tightly clasped as she continued to approach Persephone. "No, no, no, no, no… I beg of you!" Demeter fell to her knees, reaching out imploring hands. "Do not do this to me! You are my solace, my comfort, my life. I cannot bear to live without you."

Persephone's heart softened at Demeter's tears, flowing freely now as she cried into Persephone's elaborately beaded black robe.

"You must, for I am my own woman now," Persephone said, resolutely but not cruelly.

When Demeter continued to sob, Persephone looked to Zeus for help, to put an end to Demeter's futile laments, for there was no going back, but he only stared at her blankly.

He flinched when, in an instant, Hecate appeared at his side, beckoning him to lean down. He did so, but with much trepidation, for the strange and powerful witch made even the king of the gods wary. After listening to whatever Hecate whispered into his ear, he nodded, then straightened to his full height, which was immense.

"By the laws of the gods, Persephone is bound to the Underworld. There is nothing I can do about that."

Demeter groaned, burying her face deeper into Persephone's robe.

"However, being the goddess of spring, she must still usher in the rebirth that comes after death. Once her duty is complete, she may stay to revel in the light above ground with her mother, for the summer months until the harvest. Once the days grow shorter and the nights longer, let her return to her king to spend the winter months in the darkness as they please."

Demeter went still, likely knowing half the time with her daughter was better than never seeing her again. Persephone looked down at her before lifting her gaze toward Hades.

"She was wrong to try and make me stay with her, but she did so out of love, I see that now. Just as I see the choices you made were out of fear. My heart would break at having to choose one over the other, for the two kinds of love I feel, though different, are no less important to me."

Hades bowed his head. "As you have said, you are your own woman. If this compromise pleases you, I shall not reject it, nor try to amend it in anyway. The decision is yours and always will be. I will endure your absence, but I assure you I will count the seconds until you return to me, my queen."

Persephone nodded, knowing in her heart that meeting Hades in the meadow had surely been fate. The light and the dark together, forever, for one cannot exist without the other.

She bent down, wrapping a hand around Demeter's arm and urging her to stand.

"Go now, Demeter. Let me have my time here. I will see you in the spring."

CHAPTER 18

HADES TOOK IN a breath, but try as he might, he could not calm the nervous energy coursing through his limbs. His restlessness had begun three days ago, a sure sign that the short cold nights in the world above were beginning to give way to longer days.

He had started the morning in his sleeping chambers, sitting in front of a blazing fire in the hearth. When he could no longer stand it, he went to the gazing pool. What he saw in its water only confirmed the frost had given way to snow. And although the ground was now beginning to thaw, the reflection did not tell him the exact day or time his love would come back to him, which made the time harder to bear.

He would talk to her about that, so perhaps they could settle on a more precise time and date. Until then, his bones would remain restless.

Admitting defeat, he moved into the throne room where, within minutes of entering, he heard a plea from the hero Heracles.

"Alcestis already belongs to Thanatos," said Hades when the hero announced he had come to the Underworld to rescue the wife of King Admetus. "You know as well as I, a bargain struck with The Fates is a bargain that must be honored."

Apparently, Admetus had won the hand of a princess with the help of Apollo, but Apollo's twin, Artemis, thinking the man lustful and greedy, was displeased he had not given to the gods, her especially, a proper offering of thanks. Angered, the goddess left a nest of snakes in the king's marriage bed. Admetus saw this as an omen of his own demise, and rightly so, for Artemis was the goddess of the hunt.

"The man meant no offense," said Heracles. "Who among us would not make the same mistake? I dare say none of us would think to sacrifice to the gods *before* our first night of wedded bliss."

Hades tapped his fingers on the arm of his throne, annoyed the hero had involved him in such a ridiculous quest, which was purely a show of bravado.

"The meddling of the gods on Olympus is a bothersome thing, Heracles, the consequences rarely ever benefiting mortals," said Hades sharply, having little desire to get involved in the mess Apollo had made. He had other, more important things on his mind. "What would you have me do?"

"Summon the god of death here, with the princess, so I can challenge him to a fight for her!" cried Hercules. "If I win, she lives."

Hades' patience with the whole thing had worn thin. His queen would be arriving any day now, and each moment longer he had to wait felt like an eternity.

"You would challenge Thanatos?" asked Hades, though he already knew the answer. There was not a beast or man—or a god, for that matter—Heracles would not fight. He may have even challenged the king of the gods had he not been his father.

"I would, for I am the son of Zeus and the strongest of his earthly sons. I vanquished the Nemean Lion with my bare hands!" bellowed Heracles, lifting his elbow to show the cloak he wore was made of the infamous lion's skin.

Hades closed his eyes, simply so he would not roll them at the brazen, muscle-bound hero. He truly was like his father. In many respects. Hades knew full well the hero would not leave his throne room until he was allowed to fight Thanatos.

"Very well, but I must insist that you use no weapon." Hades nodded to the club Hercules held in his oversized and scarred hand. "And if you lose, neither you nor the woman will be returning to the land of the living."

Heracles nodded. "I expected no less."

Hades sighed, resigned to the fact that it was impossible to deter the hero from his mission. The woman was already in the Underworld, but if the fool thought he could wrestle her away from the god of death what did he care? In truth, he didn't care much at all. Let him take her back to the living world above.

Hades called for Thanatos to bring the woman to the throne room. After explaining the rather ridiculous situation to the god of death, who agreed with enthusiasm, a wrestling match ensued.

The fight went on for hours, with Heracles first gaining the upper hand, then Thanatos. No longer able to remain still, Hades left them to their battle to wander the halls and empty rooms of the palace. For how long, he did not know, but that hadn't worked either, for everywhere he went was devoid of the warmth and laughter that followed Persephone wherever she went.

At present, he found himself pacing outside the palace doors, his gaze fixed on the mighty gates beyond, waiting for the moment his queen arrived home.

How many times had he been in this position? Countless at this point. He should be immune to the agony of waiting by now, yet it never seemed to get easier. It seemed Cerberus was anxious, too, for he heard the beast's impatient whines all the way from where Hades wore a rut in the stone beneath his restless feet.

And then he saw them, the telltale signs that Persephone had indeed arrived. At first it was only green tendrils peeking through the barren ground near the gate. The shoots grew, twisting upward and increasing in size until a verdant carpet of vegetation covered the surrounding area. Tiny red buds appeared, dotting the mass of waxy leaves vining the gate, before erupting into fully bloomed roses a moment later.

Hades stilled, then inhaled deeply. The heady scent of roses filled his nostrils, and it wasn't long before his feet rushed down the wide stone steps of their own accord.

He felt the atmosphere change. It moved and bent, shifting like a desert mirage as Persephone appeared out of thin air on the arm of Hermes just beyond the massive iron gate. A small tweak of jealousy pinched at Hades as she pressed her lips to the psychopomp's cheek, but he quickly dismissed it. It was simply payment for safely escorting her into the Underworld.

The messenger god bowed his head, then lifting his hand to Hades in both greeting and farewell, he vanished.

Hades stood at the bottom of the stairs, grinning like a fool as he watched the gates swing open. His smile widened when Persephone approached Cerberus with an outstretched hand. Aways touching, freely giving her light to those who would accept it, including him.

The beast lowered all three heads, each eager for a loving stroke on the snout from the goddess. One sniffed the red fox at her heels. After confirming it was friend and not foe, Persephone tucked a bloom, retrieved from the small basket she carried with her, behind one ear of each of Cerberus's heads.

After greeting the fierce guardian of the Underworld, Persephone turned and looked for Hades. A smile overtook her face when she found him. Eyes locked on her, he fought to keep his breathing under control. The wait was over, and in just a few minutes she would be in his arms. He stepped onto the last stone in the long path leading from the gate to the palace stairs.

Their homecoming ritual—those who lived aboveground called it the autumn equinox—was his favorite part.

Persephone quickly made her way from Cerberus to the beginning of the path, just as eager to begin as Hades. He swallowed hard, barely able to resist closing the distance between them then and there. Instead, he composed himself as she positioned herself on the first stone, determined to complete their custom.

Following her lead, they moved toward one another in unison, and with a slow and steady pace, they continued walking. Tall grass and blooms of all sorts spread across the courtyard with each step Persephone took. Before long, a meadow sprang up around them, its wispy grass swaying in the twilight.

When they were only feet apart, Persephone quickened her pace, dropping the basket. Hades quickened his pace, too, opening his arms wide for her, already smelling the remnants of harvest spices—cinnamon, cloves, and nutmeg—that lingered from her time above ground.

They both cried out in joy when she launched herself at him. He caught her, as he promised he always would, and held on tightly as he swung her around. He did not kiss her, not yet, for now all he wanted most was to bury his face into her sweet-smelling hair and whisper how much the darkness had missed the light.

THE END

GET A PREVIEW OF THE
SORROW AND THE SEA

Amphitrite belonged to the sea. Not only because she was one of fifty daughters of the sea gods Nereus and Doris, but because she so lovingly cared for the life that dwelled within its watery depths.

She swam with purpose, on her way to a reef and its colorful residents she visited often. When she reached her destination, she stopped and admired the urchin and anemone, humming soothingly as she did. She moved along the reef, calling for the old turtle that lived there to come out of its shell. It was an ancient language, the sound more akin to singing than actual words.

She bit her lip, worried when her friend did not stir from its usual spot within the coral. She moved closer, peering into a dark crevice and calling for it again, louder this time. Just as her worry bordered on panic, it appeared, popping its head out of its hiding place.

"There you are," she said, breathing a sigh of relief before running her forefinger over the top of its head.

She was kind to all creatures, whether they possessed fin or claw, shell or scale, and though she could not explain it, felt compelled to look after them, even the fearsome sharp-toothed and powerful tentacled creatures.

Amphitrite didn't know why it was her nature to offer comfort to the inhabitants of the ocean, it just was. And so, she would swim from reef to reef, gliding along the frigid depths before rising to the shallow tide pools warmed by the sun, to make sure all was well, especially after a violent storm had rolled and thrashed the waves.

A small shudder rippled through her. She knew of the Olympian who had been given rule over the oceans by Zeus, as all who lived under the water did. He was called Poseidon, and when he raged, so did the sea. He was disgruntled quite often, and she wondered what made him so. Her father, Nereus, was always so even tempered. Nothing seemed to shake him. Perhaps it was because he was a Titan, an old god responsible for only a small part of the sea. To her, his domain seemed vast, but it must be small in comparison to King Poseidon's.

Poseidon ruled over the entirety of the sea, and every ocean, big and small, across the world. Amphitrite could not imagine what that would be like, to have such great responsibility. With so much power, was it any wonder he lost his temper sometimes?

For all the days the sea was rough, there were also many days it was calm. It was beautiful when it was the latter, making living under the waves a joy and delight. During these times of peace and tranquility, Amphitrite enjoyed the company of her many sisters, though some, she must confess, more than others.

The twins Galene and Galatea were her favorite, born close in age to Amphitrite. Galene could be bumbling at times, but in general, always seemed quite happy and optimistic. Amphitrite found she could speak to Galene about anything.

Galatea was much the same, but lately she had been spending all her time ashore. Amphitrite had heard a rumor Galatea was in love with a mortal man, but she didn't believe it. Perhaps Galatea had stumbled upon him in need of help, or he could have offered her assistance in some way. Her sisters loved to gossip. Something Amphitrite never much cared to do. Galatea had made a friend and nothing more. Why else would a nereid bother herself with the world above? Everything they truly needed was below the waves.

And then there was Calypso. Older than Amphitrite and the twins, but younger than some of the other nereids. Although she could be onerous, she wasn't always. Only when she was jealous or felt threatened in some way. It was clear she desired to occupy the thoughts and minds of everyone around her, and they had all come to accept her nature. Truth be told, Amphitrite found her more exhausting than anything.

Like any other family, her sisters possessed varying temperaments, with different combinations of traits inherited from their parents. They came by them honestly. While their father ruled with a surprisingly mild and gentle hand for a Titan, their mother, conversely, could be quite severe in both her mood and judgement. Thankfully for her children, the harshest of her brash and strong-willed nature had mellowed with age. A gentler side had emerged with each pregnancy, until she had settled into the role of nurturing mother.

That's not to say she didn't have her moments. As all goddesses must, Doris rarely showed weakness, keeping it well hidden behind a stunningly beautiful but oftentimes emotionless face.

Most of the nereids had been born kind-hearted and self-assured, but there were a few who had inherited less of these desirable qualities. Like Calypso, they were quite self-centered and spitefully jealous things, and would often target the meekest among them. Amphitrite was one of the nereids who avoided conflict. She preferred the company of sea creatures than most of her own sisters. For one thing, sea creatures were not envious of Amphitrite's hair, which was the color of a breathtaking golden dawn kissed by the ruby glow of a sunset, or that she danced so gracefully she would often garner praise from their critical mother.

That's not to say Nereus and Doris hadn't tried their best to dissuade pettiness among their daughters. But with so many, it wasn't always possible, which was why when Amphitrite was not dancing or swimming with Galene, she could be found miles away exploring some alcove or deep crag in the ocean floor, keeping company and taking care of her fellow sea creatures.

Suddenly, the clear blue water around her darkened to an icy gray, and the low rumble of

moving earth reverberated in the distance.
Amphitrite looked at the turtle with wide eyes,
but it had tucked its head back into its shell.
She stifled a panicked whimper. There was no
time to be seized by her own fear. The
creatures. She must make sure they were all
tucked safely away before racing back to the
castle.

She picked up the sea turtle and, reaching
into the crevice all the way to her elbows, she
placed it deep within the rock.

One by one, anemone closed in on
themselves and the fish that had been floating
peacefully only seconds before now frantically
darted for safety. All the while the sea swayed,
its stirring gaining speed and gathering
strength until the long leafy strands of kelp
growing around the reef whipped back and
forth violently.

"Don't be frightened," she called out,
reassuring the creatures. "His vexation will
subside soon, and all will be calm. Be well, my
friends."

Amphitrite pushed off the rock and turned
toward home. The current was strong, and her
arms quickly grew tired from straining.
Against her better judgment she changed
course, propelling herself upwards toward the

surface. If she could catch a glimpse of the King, or what had raised his ire, perhaps she could help in some way.

She broke the surface, the waves churning and tossing her about as she treaded water. *This is folly. I should not be here.* She had never seen let alone been in the presence of the King of the Sea. What could she do?

Despite this, she swam closer to shore, dragging herself onto a slippery rock to survey her surroundings. As the wind lashed at her, she saw nothing but the stormy sea punishing the land around it.

Then, without warning, an enormous crack of lightning sounded from behind her. She hauled herself around just in time to witness jagged fingers of electricity grip the horizon. The darkened sky surged with a series of flashes, illuminating clouds so ominous it made her skin prickle.

Thinking better of her foolish notion to try and bring comfort to the tumultuous King of the Sea, Amphitrite dove back into the ocean and headed toward safety.

The Author

Forever a fan of fairytales, folklore, and mythology, Kerri brings life to the mythological characters you know and love... or love to hate.

Kerri lives in Michigan with her husband, son and cat they lovingly but aptly refer to as The Maleficence. Mel for short. If Kerri isn't raking leaves or shoveling snow, she's either reading, writing or has fled her evil to-do list and fallen down an Internet rabbit hole... Or possibly just fallen and can't get up.

For news and updates about upcoming releases, sign up for Kerri's newsletter at kerrikeberly.com. For an inside look at the day in the life of a crafty crochet-addicted, DIY-loving, Greek mythology-obsessed author, follow her on Facebook, Instagram, and TikTok.

Milton Keynes UK
Ingram Content Group UK Ltd.
UKHW011907060524
442290UK00001B/28